MISSING PIECE

KINDRED SERIES BOOK ONE

LIZZIE JAMES

AUTHOR'S NOTE

First, I have to give a massive thanks to you. The reader. Without you, I wouldn't be able to do what I do. This book is for you.

Firstly, I have to thank the amazing Camila Andrews. You became the perfect Tillie and thank you so much for being my cover model. Can't wait to see you at Belfast!

I would also like to thank these amazing women – Scarlet Le Clair, Kathryn Dee, Rebecca Barber, Jade Pitman, Kathryn Stokes, Tania Shrimpton, Emma Lloyd & Louise Evans – your support and belief in me has been amazing and I'm so thankful to everything you've done for me. From the daily pimping, to facebook messages. Thank you!

To my beta readers – Scarlet Le Clair, Kathryn Dee, Lorren Smith, Paula Tarpley Genereau, Karen Bill, Amanda Williams & Emma Lloyd – thank you all so much for your honesty.

To my mother, Susan, again, thank you again for just being you.

To Carl and Stuart, my brothers. Thanks for just being there.

To the most amazing cover designer I could ever ask for. Kathryn Dee, thank you so much and I love working with you.

Eleanor Lloyd-Jones and Rachael Tonks. Thank you for being a part of this book.

Thank you to all the bloggers that have helped me and the ladies that share me. You guys rock and your support is amazing.

Hope you enjoy this book!

Love,

Lizzie x

1
———
TILLIE

Walking onto college ground after leaving high school was scary, I'm not going to lie, especially if you were me. Carrying a plastic box and one single suitcase was tragic. I didn't have any of the belongings that everyone else seemed to have. Most of the students there had parents and friends helping them to carry their stuff to their dorm rooms.

Me? I was simple, or pathetic really depending on how you looked at it.

I quickly made my way to the main office to collect my class schedule and pick up my keys for wherever I was staying.

Please give me a single dorm room.

I approached the office door just as someone pulled it open from the inside. I continued walking forward, hoping whoever was inside would be nice. I hated rude people.

That was the first bad choice of the day.

I stepped over the threshold of the doorway when my foot collided with something. Looking down over the box I was carrying, I could see it was someone's leg.

Fucking great.

I went ass over suitcase and ended up sprawled over it on the floor. Thankfully, I was dressed in leggings, so I wasn't flashing my ass to the whole world and whatever douche had tripped me over.

"Oh, my dear," an older woman's voice called. "Are you okay?"

I groaned, still slumped over my suitcase.

Just kill me now.

"Logan, be a gentleman and help the girl up." The woman had a bit of a bossy tone to her, which I kind of liked.

"I don't know," a hot male voice said from behind me. "It looks like a good view from here." He chuckled under his breath and I just knew that my ass would be starring in his dreams tonight.

I leaned back on my knees just as a hand appeared at my side. Without arguing, I took it and used him to help me to get back up on my feet. As I did, I looked up at him to give him some abuse for knocking me on my ass when it happened: mouth fell open and mind went blank.

Damn. Did all the guys around here look like him?

The guy was about two inches taller than me with dark hair. I could see what looked like the point of a star tattoo on his arm beneath the sleeve of his t-shirt.

He must have read the look on my face when he smirked. He leaned over and pressed his finger underneath my chin, lifting it up to close my mouth.

How embarrassing!

"It's all right, darlin'," he mocked. "Everyone wants me." He winked and turned around, leaving me with a receptionist that was no doubt gawking at the both of us.

I shook my head, grabbing my suitcase and box, dropping it on the floor by the counter.

"Are you okay?" she asked, looking over her glasses at me.

I wanted to laugh at the look of concern on her face. I nodded, giving her a tight smile. "I've come to collect my class schedule and the keys to my dorm room."

"Oh, right," she said, flustered. "What's the name?"

"Tillie Jacobs," I replied.

Please give me a single.

Looking around at the walls, it was obvious that this was a football school. Just like my research had shown. All around the room, there were pictures of the team and their cheer squad throughout the years hung the whole way around the room.

I looked back to the receptionist, frowning when I realized she was still looking for my name in whatever filing system she had. Surely the letter J wasn't that hard to find.

"Here we are," she smiled. The smile didn't stay on her face for long, though.

"Everything okay?"

"Well..." She wouldn't look at me for some reason. She slid a form across the counter toward me. "There seems to be a problem with your transcript."

"Problem?" I asked meekly. I took a step closer so I could try to see whatever she was reading on the form.

Her finger pointed to the section where my name was, and I wanted to groan. I had filled the entire form in blue ink when I should have used black. However, in the housing section, there was a big blue check mark in the 'other housing already occupied' box.

"What the hell?" I shrieked, taking a closer look. "Who filled that part in?"

How could I be so stupid to mess this up?

"I assumed you did, sweetie." The look of doubt on her face had me shaking my head.

If I hadn't ticked the box and if she hadn't ticked the box, that left me up shit creek without a paddle. "So where does that leave me? I get a dorm, right?"

She turned and grabbed a pile of papers.

Watching her for a few moments, I began to worry. Where the hell would I be staying for the next school year? She looked up at me and I knew that whatever she was about to say was going to be bad.

"I'm sorry to say, all available dorms have been assigned to students." She cringed when she said it. I couldn't be angry at her. It wasn't her fault. I just wanted to disappear into a big hole.

"So, I have nowhere to go?" I was trying hard not to panic, but from the look of sympathy on her face, it was obvious I was failing.

"The only thing I can advise is to apply to a sorority house."

She had to be fucking kidding. Me, Tillie Jacobs, apply to be a pledge at a prissy sorority house? Hell would have to freeze over first.

I nodded, letting her think that was my decision.

Quickly grabbing my suitcase, I exited her office sighing loudly. I knew I should have let Dad come with me. But no. I had to be my stupid, independent self.

Looking around outside, I tried searching for someone of authority. There was sure to be someone that could help me escape my fate as a stupid sorority slut.

Leaning against the wall outside was the guy I'd clumsily tripped over. Logan, was it? I was never attracted to the bad boy, tattooed type but I couldn't deny he was good looking. I must have stared at him for a little too long when he cocked his eyebrow at me.

"What's the problem, sugar?" He smirked cockily at me, probably assuming that I was checking him out, which I obviously was.

"Nothing." I shook my head, dreading my next words. "Do you know where the nearest sorority house is?" I shuffled my feet, fidgeting on the spot.

He smirked, taking a drag on his cigarette. His eyes slowly trailed down my body and back up before he bothered to reply. "You don't look like sorority material." He chuckled, flicking his cigarette to the floor before stubbing it out with his shoe.

I wrinkled my nose in disgust at his actions. I had no problem with smokers, but people who threw their rubbish on the floor really wound me up.

Before I could say anything, he bent down and picked the stub up. He moved a few steps away, depositing the stub in the bin. "So," he said, turning back to face me. "Why are you looking for a sorority?"

I cringed, wanting nothing more than to avoid this conversation but it obviously wasn't going to happen. "I kind of messed up my admission form." I couldn't look at him, so I stared at the tree behind him.

"What do you mean by 'kind of'?" His head ducked into my line of sight and he had the widest grin on his face. He must have thought I was a complete idiot.

"I didn't fill the housing section in right, okay?" I snapped at him, hating how this day was going.

He kept a straight face for all of two seconds before he threw his head back, letting out a proper belly laugh.

Just fucking great!

I narrowed my eyes, trying not to show how angry and upset I was by him laughing at me. I grabbed the handle on my suitcase and began walking away from him.

Before I could get too far, he ran after me and positioned himself in front of me, stopping me in my tracks.

"I'm sorry, I'm sorry." He looked at me with a small smirk on his face. "I didn't mean to laugh."

"Yes, you did." I wasn't a fool. If someone had told me the same, I'd probably have laughed too.

"It was funny." He grinned at me, making me roll my eyes, not sure whether it was at him or at the situation. "So, you need to find a place to stay, right?"

I appreciated him trying to change the subject. Today had to get better.

I nodded, hoping like hell he had another option. It had never been a part of my plan to become besties with sorority sisters.

He grabbed the handle of my suitcase and moved it toward him. Taking a few steps, he nodded his head toward the path and I quickly fell into sync with him.

"So, I can either point you in the direction of our sororities or I can give you another option."

"What is it?" I eagerly asked. "I'll take anything."

"Well, I have a neighbour. She's an older lady, who can rent you a room. She's cool but will probably need a little help around the house. You know, cooking, cleaning... that kind of stuff." He cocked an eyebrow at me, waiting for my reaction.

It sounded like heaven compared to what would be in store for me if I went to a sorority house. I couldn't help myself. I threw myself at him, giving him a hug. He squeezed me gently before letting me go.

We quickly made our way across town in a taxi, and I couldn't help but wonder what was waiting for me. Back home, I lived with my Dad and it was always just the two of us. I hoped this lady was nice and could help me.

After paying the taxi driver, I pulled my suitcase behind me, following Logan up the path. Staring up at the house, I was impressed: it looked like a lovely home. The walls were an oak brown and there were flowers lining the path to the house. I could see this lady was house proud. Maybe I was in luck. I was lost in my own little world when I was hit from the side. I didn't stumble too far, thankfully.

A pair of hands grabbed me, making sure I didn't fall.

I looked up coming face to face with a pair of green eyes. I couldn't shout or get angry with him for nearly knocking me off my feet. He had black, shaggy hair—a bit like you'd expect a skater boy to look like, and, looking down, I saw I was right in my assumptions. In his hand was indeed a skateboard with illuminous green splotches of paint on it.

"I'm so sorry." He grinned, releasing his hold on me. "I didn't mean to bump into you."

"That's okay." I smiled, accepting his apology. I began walking toward Logan, who immediately slid his arm over my shoulders.

"Are you visiting someone?" He cocked an eyebrow at me, probably wondering why he'd never seen me before.

"No." I shook my head. "I'm hoping to take the last spare room. Do you live here?" I pointed to the ground beneath me.

He quickly shook his head and pointed his thumb over his shoulder to the large house opposite. My eyes widened in surprise. That was one big house. Probably host to a lot of college parties.

"I'm Sammy." He smiled again, showing off his pearly white teeth.

Sammy was cute in a 'boy next door' kind of way. He grinned before Logan cleared his throat, gaining both of our attention.

"See you later, Sammy." He gave him a cocky smirk before he steered me toward the door.

When we reached the door, he unwrapped his arm from my shoulders and pushed the handle down, opening the door and walking straight in.

"Logan!" I whispered roughly, shocked at how cocky he was acting.

He rolled his eyes, reaching forward and taking my hand in his. "Come on," he chuckled. "She doesn't bite."

I widened my eyes, allowing him to drag me further into the house.

"Honey, I'm home," he mockingly called, poking his head through the door into the lounge.

"Hey, sweetie," an older, sweet voice replied to him. "There are some cookies in the kitchen for you to take over to the house."

He untangled his fingers from mine, walking to the armchair by the window. He quickly leaned down and pressed a quick kiss to her cheek.

I smiled in surprise at his actions. You'd never think this tattooed bad boy was a softie at heart.

"I brought a visitor for you." He grinned, stepping to the side so that she could see me.

She smiled in response and wasted no time in standing up to greet me.

"This is Joy. She looks after us with sugary cookies and stuff." He gave me a quick wink before continuing with his introductions. "This is Tillie. She's a new friend of mine." He took a few steps away from Joy and stood back at my side. "I have a favor to ask."

She never stopped smiling at him. "What's the problem?" Her eyes flickered between Logan and me. I could see from the look on her face that she adored this boy.

"So, Tillie here has kind of messed up her application..." He rolled his eyes mockingly. "Short story: she doesn't have a dorm room."

Her face broke out into a sympathetic expression at his words. "Oh, you poor thing." She quickly stepped toward me and wrapped her arms around me.

I hugged her back, allowing her to rock me from side

to side. My eyes met Logan's and he gave me a goofy grin, pushing his thumbs up. I rolled my eyes at how silly he was.

"Well, let's get you settled then." She pulled back from me, looking me in the eyes. "You're welcome to stay here, sweet girl."

My eyes widened in shock at how quickly she was ready to take me in to her home as a guest. "I can pay you rent. I'll get a part time job and do whatever I can to help out." I was babbling at that point. I wouldn't have been surprised if she hadn't understood me.

"Oh, hush," she admonished me. "If you can help with the shopping and help me around the house, that's all I ask."

I shook my head. This was too much. I couldn't just take a room off this kind lady and not even offer any money in payment.

"Can I please pay you rent?" I'd clean the house every day if she needed it but taking a room for free. I just couldn't do that.

"Absolutely not." She moved closer to me, taking my hands in hers. "Please let me help you." She nodded her head towards Logan, a cheeky smile gracing her face. "This one over here." She shook her head. "Those boys across the road have become like family. They're always over here raiding my cupboards for cookies."

I giggled at the thought of Logan on a sugar-high.

"I need the extra help around here." She winked at me, reminding me so much of my own grand-mother that passed away a few years ago.

I nodded my head, reluctantly giving in. I'd find a

way to repay her. Even if it was only through grocery shopping. "Thank you so much!" I enthused, tightening my grip on her hands.

She laughed at my enthusiasm, shaking her head. She must have thought I was crazy. "Logan, bring her case upstairs," she gently ordered him.

He chuckled, taking my case from me, and followed her up the stairs.

I couldn't help but stare at Logan's ass the whole way up.

Joy led the way into the guest bedroom on the top of the stairs, and I gasped at the sight: bright blue walls greeted me with a double bed in the corner and an oak desk on the other side. It had a walk-in closet and an ensuite bathroom.

"So, this will be your room, dear, and I'll be across the way from you." She pointed to the closed door at the other end of the hall.

I nodded, still in a daze that I had somewhere to live. I had been starting to think I'd have to call home and borrow even more cash off Dad.

"Logan, let's go downstairs and pack those cookies up and you can take them home for the boys."

"See you later, darling." He gave me a wink and followed Joy from the room.

"Thank you, Logan." I called after him.

Looking around the room, I couldn't help but do a happy dance on the spot. Logan was a lifesaver.

I fell back on the bed, letting my legs dangle over the edge.

Thankfully, Logan and Joy both saved the day.

AS THE DAYS PASSED, Joy and I fell into a comfortable routine. It almost felt as though we had known each other for weeks instead of days.

Making my way to campus, I laughed to myself as I remembered Joy bustling around that morning. Before I had even come downstairs, she had packed me a sandwich for lunch. It sounds horrible to say, but I think she needed company just as much as I needed her. I'd offered to have a police check done on me, but she just rolled her eyes. She was a very stubborn woman.

Leaving the art building hours later, I wanted to groan. Considering it was the first class of the semester, the professor hadn't taken it easy: he wanted an essay done in the next week discussing what art meant to us and how it had been affected by the digital age. He obviously hated us already.

Walking into the cafeteria, my eyes slowly moved over everyone. It was a busy place. I thought college would be different from high school, but looking around I couldn't help but notice it looked very much the same. Jocks, cheerleaders, goths... They were all mingling in their groups.

My eyes were quickly drawn toward a girl from my art class who was waving her arm around trying to get my attention. Her name was Bex and she was like my complete opposite. She hated landscapes and preferred live drawings and I was the other way. I was an art geek and looked like it whereas she looked like she should be walking a catwalk. I smiled at her and gave her a small wave, my feet quickly taking me in her direction at the back of the room.

When I was only a few tables away, I shrieked as I was pulled to the side and landed on someone's lap. Before I could get appropriately angry, a pair of arms quickly wound around me, squeezing me to them.

"Where have you been hiding?" Logan looked down at me, giving me a cheeky wink. "Was starting to think you were avoiding me."

I laughed at his comment. "I've been meaning to come over to see you." I forced myself to keep looking at him. I knew he was at a full table and I could feel more than one set of eyes on me.

"We're having a house party on the weekend. Come over and meet everyone, okay?" His green eyes twinkled with mischief.

"I promise." I smiled at him, not being able to refuse him.

His arms slowly unwound from around me, allowing me to move.

As I began to walk away, I couldn't stop it. My eyes wandered back, locking on to Logan's frame. His back was already turned and there were several people at his table already laughing at whatever he was saying. I could see he was obviously the life of the party.

I moved my gaze to the guy sitting next to him. He was staring at me with one of the sexiest smiles on his face. I turned back around, surprised and joined Bex at her table and quickly fell into conversation about pastels and shadows.

"Bex," I whispered. "Who's that guy sat over there?"

She looked over my shoulder, grinning. "You mean the one currently staring at you like he wants to eat you for dessert?"

I widened my eyes in shock at her.

She rolled her eyes at my reaction. She turned and dunked a fry in her tub of sauce before turning back to me. "That's Johnny Baker. He's the star of the football team." She leaned closer to me and whispered in my ear. "He can't take his hands off you!"

I spun around, completely shocked. My eyes met his before he gave me a quick wink and turned in his seat.

Damn! He really was cute.

2

JOHNNY

HEADING OUT OF THE HOUSE, I PLUGGED MY earbuds in and set off for my early morning run. It was a pattern I had fallen in to since attending as a football student. I shook my head. No. Not a football student. I was THE football student.

On game day, all eyes were on me and my ability to lead our team to victory.

Around college, I looked like the easy-going, cocky prick. That's what I let everyone see and think of me, but inside... inside was a different story completely. I felt the pressure from the whole campus and I carried every single team member's hopes and dreams on my shoulders. It was a heavy burden to wear but I was the only one that could do it. Getting my head into a routine was the best way I knew how to handle it. Keeping my grades up to a B average, keeping my fitness routine to an above average level and hanging out with the boys was the only way I knew how to operate.

That and receiving more than my fair share of female attention.

It's not like I was a player or anything. It was just normal to be the one that the ladies would flock to. It didn't matter anyway. It wasn't like anyone met the love of their life in college. Right?

Jogging down the street, I could have sighed in bliss. It was my favorite part of the day: no people, no passing cars and no flirtatious looks—just me and the cold air.

After doing a quick circuit of the campus and after my second turn around the football field, I began making my way back home. Jogging up the street, I slowed my pace. Looking ahead, I could see my neighbour, Joy, out in her garden, no doubt checking on her flowers.

For as long as I had lived there, she had been fascinated by her garden. From my very first day of college, she had taken me in as a part of her family. She was almost like a grandmother to me these days. Her kindness had even reached over into our house and all the boys had come to think fondly of her.

"Good morning, beautiful." I stopped outside her garden wall, leaning my arms on top. As she turned to look at me, I gave her a cheeky wink.

She smiled warmly at me, making her way closer. "How are we doing, kid?" she asked, leaning her weight against the wall from her side.

"Nothing much." I shrugged my shoulders dismissively, acting my cocky, confident self. "Just been for a run so, going to go and get ready for class."

"You found yourself a girl yet, Johnny?" She cocked her eyebrow at me.

I rolled my eyes, laughing at the fake stern expression on her face. "Why settle for one when you can have several?" I grinned cheekily at her, knowing how much she would hate my reply.

"That brother of yours arrived yet?" Her eyes flickered over to look at my house. "I hope you're looking after him."

I nodded, secretly loving that she was already worrying about him. "Yeah, Sammy's already on the team as well." I frowned when I saw one of her upstairs lights turn on.

"You got company?" I tried not to act like an ass, but I knew I sounded like I was pissed off. I tried not to be, but if she had a man in there, he and I needed a chat. Like I said, she was like a grandmother to me and no way was he getting comfortable in that house without me checking out if he was genuine enough for Joy.

She rolled her eyes at me, smirking. "It's my new house guest." She couldn't hide the smile on her face, even if she was trying to. "She's started college and needed a place to stay."

I relaxed my shoulders, rolling the tension out. "Well, that's okay then, I guess."

"I'm glad I have your permission." She laughed, shaking her head at me.

"I hope she's helping you out with the house." I nodded my head at the house. I knew I was being nosey, but I didn't want a lazy sponger abusing Joy's good nature.

She chuckled, turning away from me. "See you later, Johnny."

"I'll bring Sammy over to meet you," I called after her.

She waved her hand at me, making her way inside the house.

I sighed, hating that she might feel like I'd overstepped the line. I'd make it up to her later by taking Sammy over to see her.

Heading inside the house, I took a quick shower and later made my way down to the kitchen. I rolled my eyes at how empty it was. The boys still had their asses lying in bed. Classes started in just over an hour and they were still snoring the day away.

I quickly poured myself a bowl of cereal, scoffing it down with a glass of orange juice.

My attention was quickly diverted when I saw Sammy stumble through the doorway dressed in only his yankee shorts. I laughed at how hungover he looked. Logan followed behind him, looking a lot better.

Sammy was my younger brother and had just started his first year of college. He had already attended three rounds of try-outs and would be starting his college football career as a reserve. He was gutted with that position. He had his heart set on being on the starting team. Sammy just hadn't learned the lesson that nothing in life came easy. If he wanted it as badly as I knew he did, the coach would see that. He just had to wait for the opportunity to prove it.

"Too much booze last night, Sammy?" I mocked, grinning cheekily at him.

"Whatever." He chuckled, taking the dig respectfully.

I laughed, leaving them in the kitchen, grabbing my bag from the lounge.

Hours later, I was finally exiting Marketing 101 and decided to make my way to the cafeteria to hang out with the boys. My eyes landed on Logan sitting at a table all on his lonesome.

Ever since Sammy and Logan had been little, they went everywhere together. Wherever you found one, the other was never far behind.

Logan was Sammy's best friend, although he was a year older than him. I guess you could've said Logan was a bit of a rebel. He was usually found hanging with the skater crowd. Although, due to his bad boy reputation and the fact that his arms were completely covered in ink, you'd assume he was from the wrong side of the tracks. He was; but Logan was also a family man. Family meant everything to him

I quickly made my way over to him, and, before I knew it, we were joined by some of our friends.

After a while, I zoned out of the conversation and began peeling the crusts off my sandwich. I could never stand to eat them. My attention was quickly diverted when Logan suddenly pulled a young girl down into his lap.

Logan had always been a 'love them and leave them' kind of guy.

My eyes quickly landed on her, and I couldn't look away.

She was beautiful.

She wasn't my normal type of girl, but there was something else about her. This wasn't a girl you could just love and leave. She had that spark in her eyes that would keep you going back for more.

As I watched Logan talk to her, I noticed how obviously comfortable she was in his arms. There was no awkwardness or hesitation. It was like they had been doing this for weeks.

I shook my head at the path my thoughts were taking but froze when I saw where his hands were. One was wrapped around her back, supporting her and the other was resting on her leg, just above her knee. My fists tensed in response and I couldn't deny the unmistakable coil of jealousy that fizzled through my veins.

Thankfully, before I made a complete ass of myself, she slowly peeled herself from Logan's arms and began making her way across to the table she was obviously originally aiming for.

"As you can see," he chuckled, when she was out of earshot, "all the ladies want me." He grinned mockingly, making most of the table erupt in laughter.

"So, who's that?" I nodded my head toward her, needing to know her story and more importantly, why the hell hadn't I ever seen her around campus before.

"Dude, that's Tillie." He threw a chip in his mouth before continuing. "She just moved here. She's a freshman art student."

I frowned in confusion, causing him to roll his eyes mockingly, almost implying there was something wrong with art students.

"Anyway," he continued, "she's living across the street from us. She moved in with Joy and..." He shrugged his shoulders dismissively. "That's all I know really."

Huh. I wanted to laugh at myself. This morning I was getting all bent out of shape at the thought that Joy might have had a man in her home and the whole time it was the little five feet of Tillie. Joy must have had a good laugh at me.

I nodded, taking Logan's words in. I looked back to get another glimpse of her and noticed she was sitting with a few of her friends. I couldn't deny that she was gorgeous. She had long, light brown hair that came to the middle of her back. She had a slim figure and the cutest smile on her face. Whilst I watched her laugh at whatever her friends were saying, her nose would crinkle up as though she was going to sneeze. It was kind of cute. I'm man enough to admit my eyes had wandered down to her chest more than once.

Fuck. She was perfect.

She turned around, her beautiful, Bambi eyes meeting mine. Fuck, she was beautiful. I gave her a wink before turning around.

I shook my head, bringing my attention back to the table I was sitting at. Before I could join any conversation, my attention was diverted once again when Chunk walked in.

Chunk and I had clicked from day one. We were both football addicts and we had slowly become inseparable since college started. We met at try-outs and began pushing each other at training sessions until we were moved from our reserve positions to full positions. He quickly became the team's fullback and I swiftly moved into the line-backer position. My arm had greatly improved since leaving high school. In our second year, Chunk had pushed himself to his limits and had become the captain of the team. The college had never had such a young Captain before, but the team certainly didn't suffer for it. The coach was impressed with how high the team morale was and that was all down to Chunk. If there were any issues within the team, he made sure he was aware of them. He made it his mission to make sure we were all on the same page.

He raised his hand, waving me toward him.

I frowned in confusion, clapping Logan on his shoulder. "See you later, man." I quickly met Chunk by the doorway.

"We have a problem," he said seriously.

It worried me when Chunk got all serious. He had always been the funny guy, and him and seriousness really didn't go well together.

I cocked an eyebrow at him, waiting for him to continue.

"It's Sammy." He looked tense.

I pushed past him, making my way outside. I had only gotten a few steps when I heard voices yelling and chanting one singular word: fight. There was a ring of students all yelling, and I could see three boys in the centre. Two against one. Fucking pathetic.

I jogged down the steps, pushing my way through the crowd. Some moved. Some didn't. It didn't matter. I quickly made it to the centre of the ring just in time for one of the cowards to grab Sammy while the other punched him straight in the jaw. Fucking idiots.

I didn't hesitate. I grabbed the back of the jackass' jacket, who obviously loved punching my little brother in the face, and threw him backwards so that he landed behind me. The other one quickly let Sammy go, raised his hands and backed away from him.

"Right, people!" Chunk yelled behind me. "Show's over. Fuck off elsewhere."

I took Sammy's chin in my hand, gently turning his face up to me and winced at the sight that greeted me. He had a cut on his bottom lip and his eye would be swollen tomorrow. "What happened?" I frowned, hating seeing these marks on him.

He yanked his face away from my grasp, kicking the ground with his sneaker. "Fucking losers started it!" he snapped, nodding his head toward the boys as they walked away from us.

"Because...?" I cocked my eyebrow at him, waiting for whatever he was going to say.

His eyes slowly moved from mine until he was staring at the floor. His short brown hair slowly fell forward across his forehead. He shook his head, mumbling something under his breath. He whispered it so quietly that I couldn't make out what it was.

"What was that?" I ducked my head closer to his, needing to know what the problem was. I couldn't help him if I didn't know what the fuck was going on.

"It's nothing." He straightened his posture, looking back at me. "It's nothing."

I stared at him a few moments before nodding my head. I'd let it go for now. We'd definitely be having a chat later.

"How about some one-on-one before practice starts?"

He grinned, nodding his head exaggeratedly fast.

I chuckled at the change of expression on his face. Sammy loved football. I think he could throw a ball before he could even walk or run.

THE DAYS PASSED SLOWLY.

I found classes were harder this year and more intense as a junior. The professors were building the pressure. Thankfully, we didn't have to worry about any seasonal games at that point. The sports calendar didn't start until the end of October, so the team would be using the time to get our new members up to the level we expected them to be and preparing ourselves for the first game of the season.

Walking into the house after a long day of Finance and Economics, I wanted nothing more than to just collapse face down on my bed. I groaned when I got inside and saw Chunk directing a few freshmen students where to set the kegs up in the kitchen. There'd obviously be no early night of chilling for me. Later tonight, this house would be party central.

Hours later, it was exactly that. Drinks were being passed around, couples were hooking up and I think some guy was already receiving a hand job in the corner of the kitchen. I laughed, tossing back another beer.

Chunk already had three ladies all over him and Sammy was currently being helped into a handstand over the keg and had a nozzle directed into his mouth. I laughed when I imagined how he would be feeling in the morning. I looked around the room, taking stock of who was there when my eyes landed on Logan. That boy was a party animal. He had his back to the room and no doubt had a girl already pressed against the wall. Whoever she was would have trouble with him. He was like flavour of the month around here.

Walking past the main door to the house, I planned to make my way upstairs to make sure my room was locked. No way was I going to have a couple fucking on my bed. That shit is disgusting. I stopped when I heard a hard bang on the door.

I frowned, confused.

Who the fuck knocks on the door at a party? The idiots can just walk on in.

I shook my head, grasping the door handle and swinging it open. The frown quickly left my face when I saw who it was.

Tillie.

She stood there in a pair of leggings, white tank top with some paint stains on and a small brown cardigan. She obviously wasn't dressed for a party but there she was.

My eyes quickly moved past her tits until they met her eyes. She had the sexiest, pissed off expression on her face.

I took a quick swig of my beer, not bothering to hide

the fact that I was obviously checking her out. "You coming in?" I asked, nodding my head behind me.

She looked disgusted by my question, but it still didn't stop my eyes from once more wandering down to her chest. She quickly crossed her arms, blocking my view.

"No!" she snapped, fidgeting on the spot. "I want you to turn the music down."

Seriously? She was here to complain. She'd barely been here five fucking seconds and here she was trying to tell me what to do.

"Look," she said, pointing across the street to Joy's house. All the lights were on and I could see Joy looking through her curtains. "She'd never come over here and complain but she shouldn't have to put up with this." She gestured to the doorway.

"Okay." I nodded my head, indicating that I understood. "I'll turn it down."

"Thank you."

She went to turn away but froze when I continued.

"As long as you'll come in and have a drink." I smirked at her, knowing I would win this battle. It was obvious she cared for Joy and I knew she'd do this.

She cocked her eyebrow at me, not looking impressed by my response. I guess parties really weren't her thing.

"Excuse me?"

Now she looked even more pissed off.

"Just one drink," I said, holding my left index finger up. If this was the only way I could get her to myself for a few minutes, I'd happily do it.

She narrowed her eyes at me in response before her

expression suddenly cleared. "Fine." She stomped her way past me and headed straight for the kitchen. She wasted no time in grabbing the nozzle that Sammy had been sucking on earlier and filled her cup up. She turned to face me and gave me a bright smile.

I frowned, confused by her expression. It may have looked like a bright and happy smile, but I wasn't that stupid. She moved past me and walked straight up to Sammy and Logan. Within seconds, Logan had slung his arm around her shoulders, bringing her into his conversation with Sammy.

I lifted myself up on to the worktop, watching the three of them. It hadn't exactly gone to plan. Right now, she was supposed to be throwing herself at me, like the rest of them around here.

I brought the bottle back to my lips, gulping it down, and then, tossing it into the bin, I walked closer to them, determined to try to steal her away from them. Whoever knew I'd be outdone by my geeky younger brother and his friend.

Stopping next to her, I looked down, but her attention was completely focused on Logan. I rolled my eyes, making Sammy chuckle. Logan looked at me, grinning cockily. He assumed this was a win, but I was just getting started. She turned to me, her eyes widening when she saw how close to her I was standing.

I opened my mouth to ask how her classes were going, when she suddenly brought the paper cup to her lips and took three gulps. She crumbled the paper cup up and offered it to me, and, like a fool, I took it.

She smirked at me and tapped me mockingly on the chest as she walked away. "Turn it down, jock!"

I laughed at the cockiness oozing from her, making Sammy and Logan laugh. They were completely drunk.

Watching her ass walk away from me, I knew one thing was certain: Tillie would be mine, whether she knew it or not.

3

———

TILLIE

Walking back to Joy's house, I smirked at Johnny's face as I left. I was pretty sure he thought he would have me all hung up on his junk like the rest of the brainless bimbos around here. He'd have a long wait until I fell into his bed.

As I entered the house, Joy paused in her knitting. She looked worried and I hated seeing that expression on her face.

I smiled warmly at her, hoping to alleviate her worries. "They're going to turn it down." I pointed my thumb behind me.

I walked into the kitchen, turning the kettle on and adding some chocolate powder to a mug and a teabag in one for Joy. I could still hear the music blasting. If anything, I could have sworn it'd gone up.

I tapped my fingers against the worktop, my patience starting to thin. I cocked my head, listening. Slowly the music started to go down. It wasn't low, but it was no longer pounding through the windows. I quickly poured the drinks and took them in. Joy was happily knitting again so I took my place back on the floor, resuming my sketch of her.

This was my passion.

I normally preferred doing landscapes, but live drawing was something I knew I would have to practice. I loved capturing emotions on people's faces and I don't think I'd seen Joy look as happy as she did right then. In her spare time, she knitted baby hats and mittens for the local hospital. She never charged for it, but she would often go in and chat with the mothers and have a baby cuddle in return. She loved it.

SITTING in the campus gardens the next day, I was tense. I had my first oil painting class that afternoon and I was nervous. I'd never experimented with paints before and new things always made me nervous. I huffed, leaning my weight back until I was lying down. Taking some deep breaths, I tried coaching myself to remain calm.

Breathe in. Breathe out.

In. Out.

My nerves settled, and I began to breathe normally again. It was so comfortable lying there that I didn't want to get up. Opening my eyes slowly, I frowned at the sight that greeted me. Logan stood by my head, looking down at me.

"She kick you out already?" He grinned, teasing me.

I rolled my eyes and held my hands up for him to help me up. "Not yet," I replied when I was back on my feet. "I thought you'd have more faith in me than that." I smirked, letting him off the hook. Grabbing my backpack, I started walking toward the path that would lead me to my art class.

Logan quickly fell into sync beside me, slinging his arm over my shoulders. "So," he started, keeping his eyes on the path. "I heard a rumor that you and Johnny may have a thing for each other."

I laughed, tossing my head back against his arm. "And what idiot told you that?" I cocked my eyebrow at him, waiting for a response. "We've only hung out a few times and that's always been with other people around." I giggled, wondering what the hell he could be thinking.

"That one." He nodded his head forward.

My eyes quickly followed the path and landed on Sammy. Before I could question Logan any further, I realized we had arrived in front of my class.

"Just don't go falling in love with him. Okay?" He grinned at me. "Or me. We have a habit of breaking the female population's hearts"

I laughed, at a loss what to say. "Why do I have to fall in love with anyone? I'm perfectly okay all by myself."

"I know." He nodded his head, raising his hands in defense. "It's just, ladies have a habit of getting all girly feelings for me." He rolled his eyes. "And you're cool. I like that we can just hang out."

It might have sounded like he was joking, but there was a hint of seriousness on his face he didn't try to hide.

I nodded, turned and walked away.

All through class, I didn't even bother to try to pay attention; I was too absorbed in Logan's parting words.

Was he serious and gently trying to warn me off? Or was he worried that I was starting to become too familiar with him?

I shook my head, confused: Logan was a friend; that was all. I didn't have many of those in my life and I knew that Logan was one of the good ones. He didn't have to worry about any romantic feelings developing there.

My mind then wandered to his comment about Johnny. Was he worried? And more importantly, why the hell did he bring it up?

To be honest, I had no romantic interest in anyone. Especially not Johnny. I was new, but I'd been there long enough to hear the rumors. Johnny was off limits to anyone that didn't want their heart trampled on. He had a different girl every weekend and I had no interest in becoming a notch on his bed post.

Class ended, and I shook my head at how much attention I didn't pay. I'd make sure to get caught up with the notes before next class.

On my way home, I popped into the grocery store to get the groceries that Joy had written down on the list she'd stuck to the fridge that morning.

I chuckled to myself when I read over what she had written at the bottom: something chocolatey for a girly night in.

I chose chocolate ice cream and a pack of wafer sticks. She may have looked elderly, but Joy was young at heart.

Walking into the house once I was finished, I

frowned when I heard how silent it was. I called her name on the way to the kitchen just in case she was upstairs.

No response.

Looking at the fridge, I saw she had left me a note.

Gone to drop some blankets off at the hospital. Won't be long.

After packing the groceries away, I decided a shower was needed before starting on the essay that was due by Monday.

Entering my bedroom, I slid my sneakers and jeans off and pulled my t-shirt off. Unclasping my bra, my eyes trailed to the window. I froze for a few seconds before shrieking and running to the side so that I was out of view of the window, hiding behind the curtain.

What a perv!

Johnny was standing on his patio with a big smirk on his face, tossing a football up and down in the air. He obviously saw the strip tease that I had performed for him, completely unaware.

I groaned, grabbing my towel and wrapping it around me before heading for the bathroom.

After taking a shower, I felt a little calmer. Thankfully, he hadn't seen everything. I needed to remember to close the curtains.

Drying my hair, I could hear Joy moving around downstairs. Tossing my hair in a bun, I made my way downstairs and headed for the kitchen.

I froze at the doorway when I saw who she was with.

Could my day get any worse?

Johnny was sitting at the table having a cup of tea with her, chatting her ear off.

My eyes narrowed at him, making him smirk at me in response.

"There she is." Joy greeted me, standing up and giving me a small hug and a kiss on the cheek. "We were just talking about you, sweetie."

"You were?" I asked surprised.

She turned to take her seat again and I gave Johnny a pointed look, trying to threaten him silently.

I took a vacant seat opposite Johnny but next to Joy.

"Yes." She nodded. "I was just telling Johnny how much of a help you've been living here with me."

I smiled, relaxed. I wanted to mentally roll my eyes at myself. What was I expecting him to say to her? That I'd been flashing myself to him from across the street?

"So, what are you doing here, Johnny?" I knew my tone wasn't polite, but did he really have to be over here after perving at me?

He smiled innocently, acting like the perfect little schoolboy. "I was just asking Joy if she still needed her upstairs landing decorated." His eyes left me to glance at Joy. "The boys and I can come over and do it for you."

"Such a sweet boy." She was crooning at him now. "I would like it done," she replied, nodding her head. "I have some color charts here somewhere." She stood up and moved behind Johnny to search in the drawer. "I'd like a nice color as we have a lovely view. Maybe something cream or coffee colored."

"Gorgeous view," Johnny replied, smirking. His eyes remained on me, slowly flickering down to my chest and back up.

I crossed my arms, shocked he was doing that with Joy around. I subtly nodded my head toward Joy. He rolled his eyes, probably thinking I was completely crazy.

Joy quickly joined us back at the table, showing off her color charts to Johnny.

I leaned over, pressing a quick kiss to Joy's cheek and left them to their discussion. Jogging up the stairs, I quickly changed into a fresh pair of jeans and top, grabbing my hoodie and sketch pad.

"I'm going out for an hour," I called as I left the house.

Turning left, I headed up the street in the opposite direction to the campus. Looking around, I was hoping something would catch my eye—something new and fresh I could escape into.

I was several blocks away when I heard voices yelling and laughing and wheels moving. It almost sounded like wheels of a bicycle. Turning the corner, I could see several large ramps behind a fence. Just behind, there was a beautiful green field.

Jogging across the street, I entered through the gate and made myself comfortable against a large oak tree. From here, I had the perfect view of what I could now see were skaters hanging out there, performing flips and jumps.

Looking up, I focused on one of the boys with a skateboard. He was standing, it would seem, at the beginning of the ramp track, holding his arms out and widening his stance, no doubt demonstrating to the younger skaters how to stand and position their arms.

I smiled at how sweet this action was.

It felt like I had only been drawing for a few moments, but it was obviously much longer than that when compared to the amount of detail I had managed to get down.

I saw something move to the side of me that caught my attention. I turned my head and jumped out of my skin. Sammy was sitting right there. How the hell had he managed to sneak up on me?

I laughed, holding my hand to my chest.

"I'm so sorry," he apologized, looking at me with a concerned expression. "I didn't mean to startle you." He chuckled under his breath with a faint blush on his cheeks.

"That's okay." I smiled warmly at him, hoping to make him feel better. "How are you?" I hadn't really had much of a chance to speak to Sammy, but he seemed nice enough.

Looking at his profile, I smiled at how he looked. He was a few inches taller than me with short brown hair; longer at the front. When he bent forward, it'd flop forward. His smile was dangerous. He had the sweetest smile. He was super cute in the 'boy next door' kind of way.

"Can't complain." He shrugged his shoulders dismissively. His eyes slowly trailed down to look at my sketch. "You're pretty good." He pointed his finger at the scenery behind the figure in my sketch.

"Thanks." I smiled, embarrassed. I still wasn't

comfortable at accepting compliments on my art. It was something I hoped to get used to.

His eyes slowly trailed back to watch the skaters and I half-heartedly focused back on my sketch. I was never able to sketch if I had company— with the exception of Joy—so it didn't have my full attention, but I managed to get some more done.

My eyes trailed over to Sammy, noticing how much he was fidgeting. He kept clenching his hands into fists as though he was nervous. Surely, he wasn't nervous because of me.

Looking up at his face, I saw he was looking at the exact same place I had been looking since arriving: the skate instructor.

Sammy had a blush on his face and he kept nibbling on his bottom lip. Was Sammy interested in him? He was looking at him the same way that half of the campus looked at his brother.

"Everything okay?" I asked. I pressed my hand to his, interfering with his hand that was repeatedly clenching.

His posture straightened at the contact, causing a frown to take over his face. He cleared his throat, nodding his head. "Sure." He gave me a tense smile. "Yeah, I'm good."

I gave him a gentle smile, hoping he truly was okay.

It was moments later before he started fidgeting again, only this time, he had an apple in his hands. I grinned at the loud crunch that came from him.

Shading in the shadow details of my subject, I smiled in surprise at how comfortable sitting with Sammy was. He seemed fine with no constant conversation. Personally, I couldn't stand those people that had to always have something to say. They stressed me out.

Finishing my sketch, I scribbled my name at the bottom right with the date and held it up. "Ta dah!" I chirped, holding it up for Sammy to view.

His eyes widened, taking my sketch pad from me. His eyes flickered between the sketch and subject, his mouth opening several times

I cringed, secretly loving and hating the shocked expression on his face.

"It's so accurate!" he enthused, still looking between the drawing and subject. He handed the sketch pad back to me and I wasted no time in ripping it from the binder.

I began to crumple it up in my hand, intending to throw it in the first bin I came to.

"What are you doing?" he yelled, shocked at my actions.

I shrugged my shoulders, stopping my actions. "I don't really want to keep a picture of a random stranger on my wall," I replied sarcastically. I chuckled, hoping to take the sting out of my words. I stood up, resuming my scrunching up of the paper.

Sammy smiled at me and held his hand out for the paper. I frowned, confused. He took it, making a quick jog to the bin.

I bent down, grabbing my pencil and shoving it in my jeans pocket. Sammy joined me as I exited the park, falling in step with me. We fell into a comfortable silence as we strolled home, both lost in our own thoughts, I guess.

As we got further up our street, I chuckled as I saw a

few boys outside Sammy's house throwing a football back and forth to each other.

Boys and their toys.

"So, when is your first game?" I asked, nodding my head toward them.

Sammy followed my line of sight, grinning when he saw them. "Not until the end of October." He frowned, the smile vanishing from his face. "I'm just a reserve."

I frowned with him. He seemed gutted; it was obvious he was a lover of the game and he had to sit on that bench, just waiting to be called up.

"You'll get there." I gave a pathetically gentle punch to his arm, trying to show my support.

We were outside Joy's house and I stared down at my sneakers, feeling awkward. Did I give him a hug? Shake his hand? I hated being social with people.

I raised my hand, opting for a wave but my attention was quickly taken when Logan threw the ball in our direction. He called Sammy's name, but Sammy was too slow to turn to catch it in time.

I half-gasped, half-shrieked and threw my arms up to shield my head from getting hit.

Nothing happened. I wasn't knocked to the ground by the ball, and I wasn't hit by the object either.

I slowly lowered my hands and peeked up.

I gasped when I saw Johnny was standing at my side, with his arm extended in front of my face, holding the ball.

He glared across the street before looking down at me. "You okay?" he asked gently, looking concerned.

I nodded, feeling tense. If that ball had hit me in the

head, I would have been on the floor. "Y-yeah," I stuttered. I hugged my sketch pad to my chest, acting as if everything was okay.

"Be careful where you're throwing the ball!" he yelled, tossing the ball back to Logan.

"Sorry, Till," Logan called back, before resuming throwing the ball back to his team mates.

Sammy gave me a small wave and jogged across the street to join his friends.

"You sure you're okay?" Johnny cocked an eyebrow at me, as though he was expecting me to give him another answer. "You look a bit... freaked."

I gave him a warm smile. "I'm okay," I nodded, trying to inject some positivity in my tone.

"Well, I had better go." He pointed across the road. He obviously had a lot on his plate living with team mates.

I gave him a small smile before moving past him into Joy's garden.

After a few steps, I spun around. "Johnny!"

He turned, looking at me seriously.

"Thank you." It was sincere. Since I had been little, I had only ever had my Dad to look after me. It was always just me and him.

He smiled warmly at me, nodding his head before continuing his walk across the street.

I turned back, walking in to Joy's home, my new home, feeling lighter than I had since arriving here.

Maybe Johnny wasn't so bad.

Sure, he could be cocky and an asshole jock, but

beneath that... beneath that, I had a feeling there were a lot more layers than people realized.

If I was honest, if I could pick between 'Johnny: the asshole jock' or 'Johnny: the boy who stopped me getting hit by a flying ball', I'd pick the latter.

Which would be bad.

For me.

I didn't have the strength or energy to hold on to a guy like that.

I was better off alone.

4

JOHNNY

Walking home from college, I thought back to the last time Tillie and I had spoken. It had been the day Logan had almost knocked her out with that throw. She had disappeared from Joy's after my teasing. The whole time I'd browsed through the color collection, I hated the anxiety that had crawled through my veins. I hated that my teasing had made her leave her own home.

I shook my head, still angry with myself.

Since that day, I had barely seen her. Every time our paths were due to cross, she'd do a one-eighty and turn around, cross the street or just march up to someone and start talking to them. Anything she could do to avoid me, she made sure to do it.

Walking toward Joy's home, I saw that she was out fussing over her flowers, like always. Stopping outside, I leaned my arms on her garden wall, watching her pull some loose weeds up.

I coughed exaggeratedly, alerting her to my presence. "So, what are you doing?" I grinned cheekily at her.

"Just making my hedges look pretty." She smiled up at me, her eyes twinkling. She straightened up, getting to her feet and walking closer to me. "I thought you were supposed to be bringing that little brother of yours over." She cocked her eyebrow at me with a no-nonsense attitude.

I cringed, knowing she was right. I had promised. Joy probably just assumed I had forgotten but that couldn't have been further from the truth. Sitting opposite the girl that plagued every one of my thoughts and knowing she wouldn't look at me and would probably prefer Logan to be there wasn't really on my list of things to do.

"Uh, yeah, I'm sorry about that." I rubbed the back of my neck, hating lying to her. "It's just that..." I looked back at her, seeing the look of concern on her face. "Practice has been intense."

She nodded, a look of understanding coming across her face. "How about tomorrow?" she asked, smiling warmly at me. "Tillie can help me cook for us. Logan and Chunk are welcome to join us."

I mentally groaned in defeat: I could never refuse Joy but then she had to start dangling Tillie in front of me. "Tomorrow sounds good," I smiled, giving her a small wave, and jogged across the street.

Walking into the house, I heard the sound of revving engines. Chunk and Logan were racing each other on their Need for Speed game and Sammy was sitting in the corner, staring out the window, as per usual.

Ever since he had arrived at college, he'd been different. In my first year of college, I would go home for as many of the breaks as I could manage. He was always fine —still my little brother.

Lately though, something had changed in him. It was like he had this added weight on his shoulders. I wish I could blame the football or his heavy workload with his classes, but I couldn't even say that. Unfortunately, he arrived here like this.

I decided I should just bite the bullet and talk to Mom. Maybe she knew what was wrong.

I clapped my hands together loudly, gaining everyone's attention. "No plans tomorrow night, guys! Joy is expecting us for dinner."

Logan and Chunk nodded their heads, but Sammy didn't even acknowledge me.

I walked over and gently kicked his shoe. "Did you hear me?" I cocked my eyebrow at him, crossing my arms.

He nodded his head enthusiastically. "I heard." He gave me a tight smile, getting to his feet and moving past me. Seconds later he was up the stairs to his room.

I shook my head, opening the door to the cellar. Jogging down the stairs, I wanted nothing more than to just lose myself down here for a few hours—just shut the door, block it all out and disappear into the dark.

I pulled my t-shirt and jeans off, grabbing my sweats from the locker I kept down here and slid them on. Grabbing the bandage, I wrapped it around my knuckles, not really wanting any bruises to form.

Jogging from side to side, I threw my arms out in my routine pattern, warming up my muscles. My fists collided with the punching bag chained to the ceiling.

Every punch I landed, images flashed in my mind—the same images, as if they were on repeat, almost like a video that was on a constant loop.

Tillie.

Every laugh and every smile I had ever witnessed lit up in my brain. These images should have calmed me down, really. Instead, they riled me up, made me angry. Every smile, every laugh; they had always been with the same person: Logan. Always fucking Logan.

Every time I would turn my head, she'd be there, talking to him, smiling at him. Of all the people she had to get attached to, why did it have to be my fucking housemate?

I threw my fists harder at the punching bag, no longer using it as a quick hour of exercise. Anyone would swear I had Logan inside the bag the way I was hammering it.

I heard the door creak at the top of the stairs and I stopped my pounding on the bag and turned around. "What?" I snapped, unwinding the bandage from my hands and folding it in a coil. I frowned when I had no answer. I looked up, surprise filling me when I saw who it was. "Tillie?"

She was the last person I expected to see.

"Hi." She gave me a shy smile, waving her hand awkwardly at me.

We were a few yards apart but even from there, I could see her eyes trail over my sweaty chest. I liked that she was checking me out.

Her eyes flashed back up to mine, a faint blush creeping over her cheeks.

"What can I do for you?" I asked. I walked over to my locker, grabbing my discarded t-shirt and pulling it on.

If she was any other girl, I would have had her pressed up against the wall by now. Tillie was different, though. If I had to move slow with her, then that's what I'd do.

"Never mind." She shook her head, placing her hand on the bannister. "You're obviously busy." She waved her hand up and down, dismissively.

"I'm not." I cocked my eyebrow, giving her a small smile. "So?" I left the question open. Not giving her room to escape.

She sighed, sounding defeated. Her eyes trailed to the floor, avoiding my stare. She mumbled something, but I couldn't hear.

I walked closer to her, needing her to repeat it. "Sorry?"

She sighed, raising her head to meet mine. "I messed up." She swallowed loudly, nibbling on her delectable, bottom lip. "I was supposed to pick up Joy's pain medication for her back on my way home from campus and I completely forgot."

She was babbling now and talking fast.

"The only pharmacy that's open at this hour is the one on the other side of town and that's like an hour and there are no buses running and..."

"Tillie." I spoke her name calmly because I could see she was starting to panic. "Relax. We'll borrow Chunk's car."

I passed her on the stairway, inhaling her scent as I passed. Fuck. The sweet scent of vanilla and strawberries hit my senses. That would be appearing in my one-handed fantasy tonight.

As I walked into the lounge, I saw that Chunk and Logan were still in their positions, trying to ram each other off the road on the screen. "Chunk, can I borrow your car?" I asked, knowing what his answer would be already.

He turned, his eyes going from me to Tillie and then back again. "Sure, dude." He stood up, taking his keys from his pocket and tossing them at me.

"Thanks, bro." I grabbed my hoodie off the hook by the door, quickly slipping it on and nodded my head toward the door. "Ready?"

She nodded, putting her hands in her hoodie pocket and walking toward me.

"Have fun," Logan called from his seat. Not even bothering to turn around. "Don't do anything I wouldn't do." He chuckled, turning around and giving Tillie a wink.

I rolled my eyes at his immaturity but smirked when I saw Tillie's eyes widen.

I held the door open, following Tillie before jogging ahead of her, unlocking the car and holding the passenger door open for her. "After you, my lady." I mockingly bowed like a Disney prince, making her giggle.

I smiled in response, loving the sound.

Jogging around the car, I climbed into the driver seat, clipping my seat belt into place. Pulling out into traffic, I followed her directions to the other side of town. I knew where to go but I wasn't going to tell her to shut up.

I loved listening to her talk to me, even if it was only directions.

Pulling up outside the pharmacy, I waited in the car while she went inside. Minutes later, Tillie was exiting the pharmacy. She didn't get very far when a group of young boys stood in her way, blocking her path. They wasted no time in crowding her.

Getting out of the car, I marched over to her, hating the look of fear on her face. I heard them laugh before one of them reached over and touched her shoulder.

Her eyes shot to mine, cringing when he touched her. I leaned my hand forward, planning to rip him off her by the scruff of his neck when she shook her head, looking even more scared.

I clenched my fist in response, dropping my hand.

"Problem, babe?" I cocked an eyebrow at them, hoping she appreciated me not rearranging their faces.

The guy dropped his hand and they all turned to face me.

Pussies.

I curled my lip in disgust, wanting nothing more than to smash my fist into his face.

"There a reason you're touching my girl?" I glared at him, acting like the pissed off boyfriend. I held my hand out to Tillie and not even a second went by before she'd grasped it, squeezing my fingers with hers. Pulling her closer to my side, I gave them a glare. No fucker touched Tillie, especially if she didn't want to be touched.

Walking her back to the car, I noticed she had a death grip on the pharmacy paper bag. Getting in on the driver side, I turned the ignition, stopping when I noticed her hands were shaking. I leaned over, turning the heater dials and turning the air flow in her direction. "Are you cold?" I asked, turning to look at her.

She raised her hand up to wipe beneath her eye.

Tears. I fucking hated tears.

"Tillie..." I frowned, at a loss of what to say. "Don't cry."

She shook her head, turning her face away from me.

"Hey." I took her chin in my hand, turning her face back to mine. "Don't hide from me."

Tears slowly trickled down over her cheeks. Taking her face in my hands, I wiped them away, rubbing her beautiful soft skin as I did.

"Sorry," she whispered, her eyes flicking downwards.

"It's okay," I replied cockily. "It's not the first time I've had a beautiful woman crying in front of me." I winked playfully at her, making her giggle.

Driving home, I began chatting to her about the latest Star Wars trailer. From that moment, I don't think she took a breather. It was safe to say, Tillie was a massive fan. We quickly got into a debate over Han Solo or Luke Skywalker. She was Team Han the whole way whereas I had always been on Team Luke.

Pulling up outside Joy's, I smiled when I saw a look of surprise cover her face.

"Thank you so much for taking me, Johnny." She smiled over at me, unclipping her seat belt.

My chest tightened at her words, making me smile at her. "Anytime." I grinned over at her, loving the way a few loose strands from her bun had come undone, framing her beautiful face. My fingers twitched, wanting nothing more than to reach over and tuck them behind her ear. I mentally groaned, inwardly rolling my eyes at myself. Since meeting this girl, I had turned into a complete pussy. She was all I thought about. She owned me completely and didn't even realize it. "You're welcome." My eyes flicked behind her when I saw Joy making her way down the garden.

Unclipping my belt, I made my way out of the car, trying not to look as disappointed as I felt.

Damn meddling old lady.

"There you are." Joy smiled up at Tillie, wasting no time in pulling her down into a small hug.

"Don't you have any faith in me?" I grinned down at her, rolling my eyes jokingly. "I wouldn't kidnap her."

Joy chuckled, turning to me and holding her arms out for a hug.

I leaned down, returning the gesture and hugging her. Pressing a quick kiss to Joy's cheek, my eyes collided with Tillie. I loved the way her face lit up at my interaction with Joy. She liked it.

"He was a perfect gentleman, Joy," Tillie said. "He saved the day."

Joy grinned, moving back to Tillie's side and looping her arm with Tillie's.

"So, what do I get for a reward?" I smiled at Tillie, cocking my eyebrow.

She chuckled, turning to Joy, shrugging her shoulders, and she giggled when Joy narrowed her eyes.

"Maybe when you and the boys come over for dinner tomorrow evening, Tillie will have some of her chocolate orange cake waiting."

My mouth watered at the thought. This girl would be the death of me.

I held my hand out to Tillie, smiling when she slid her small one into mine.

"You've got yourself a deal."

Tillie laughed loudly as I shook her hand, squeezing softly before letting go.

She looked down at Joy with a look of adoration on her face. "Should we go in and sort this out then?" she asked, shaking the pharmacy bag.

Joy nodded, turning toward the gate.

"Good night, ladies." I nodded my head, my eyes once again going to Tillie.

"Good night, Johnny," she softly replied before stepping toward me.

I frowned at her actions before she softly placed her hands on my chest, leaned up on her tiptoes and pressed a quick kiss to my cheek. She pulled back, walking through the front garden and shutting the front door.

I walked over to the house, grinning like a goofy fucker the whole way and I don't think I had stopped smiling until I got into the house. Heading to the kitchen, I grabbed a bottle of water from the fridge.

What felt like moments later but was obviously much longer, I looked toward the door. Chunk, Logan and Sammy all had their heads poked around it, staring at me like I had three heads.

"What?" I snapped, taking a swig of the bottle.

"What the fuck is wrong with you?" Chunk chuckled, straightening up. "You're grinning like a weirdo."

I rolled my eyes, letting him take the piss. "Whatever." I moved past them, heading for the stairs. "I'm going to have an early night."

Jogging up the stairs, I groaned when I heard them laughing.

I was completely fucked.

5

TILLIE

ALL DAY, I HAD BEEN A NERVOUS WRECK. NO CLUE why, really, because I had nothing at all to be nervous about.

Okay, that was a lie. I had one reason to be nervous.

In fact, my reason to be nervous was six feet tall, smiled like Thor and made me weak in the knees.

Since starting college, Johnny had been a player, one of the jocks and basically untouchable to a girl like me, but when that boy smiled—damn—my immediate reaction was to swoon.

Looking back on my time here, anyone would think that if there was a boy I'd develop a stupid crush on, it would be Logan—I mean, he's the one that had helped me when I needed it and found a safe place for me to live —but there was just something about Logan that put me off. I don't know what it was. I couldn't put my finger on it.

But last night, when I needed someone, Johnny

hadn't hesitated. He'd dropped everything to help me. Watching the way he was with Joy also didn't help my racing pulse.

Spending my teen years under a single dad's roof, boys were never part of the equation. After Mom died, art and studies took over. I guess I'd just never found someone that made me think of them like that.

Well, that was then.

Now was a completely different story.

Now, I was completely screwed.

Looking out of the window, I could see the four boys leave their home and start making their way across the road. I breathed a sigh of relief when I saw they were dressed casually.

I was dressed the same: I had my black Empire Strikes Back t-shirt on, leggings and my blue sneakers. It took a lot for me to get fancy.

Stirring the Bolognese sauce, I hummed at the rich, tomato scent. I had been hoping to get away with just making enough lasagne for everyone, but thankfully Joy told me that Sammy was a vegetarian, so I'd opted to make a tofu Bolognese for him.

Just like last time, Logan was here. He walked straight in without knocking and I chuckled at his informality. Take him or leave him, Logan was his own unique self.

Walking to the fridge, I pulled the chocolate orange cake out that Joy had been proudly raving about the previous day to Johnny, and placing it on the worktop, I froze when I felt the heat of someone standing right behind me.

"That looks delicious," Johnny said from behind me.

I chuckled at the eagerness in his tone, and, turning around, I looked up at him.

"Did you make that just for me?" He grinned, reaching down and tucking a lock of hair behind my ear.

I blushed at the contact, leaning back from him.

"Not just for you." I grinned back, sliding the cake topper on to protect its freshness.

Moving aside, I went back to the stove, keeping my attention on that instead of the distraction behind me.

"I'll leave you to it and go and sit with Joy." He smiled at me, leaving me in the kitchen.

It was going to be a long night.

***

"THAT WAS the best lasagne I think I have ever tasted," Chunk enthused, leaning back and rubbing his stomach.

"The food was lovely. Thank you, Tillie," Sammy said, next to me.

I blushed, not expecting any praise at all. "You're welcome." I smiled at him, receiving one back. "I'll tub the rest of it up for you and you can take it home if you like?"

He nodded, giving me a cheeky grin.

I looked over at Johnny and he gave me a smile, silently mouthing the words 'thank you' at me.

I stood up, grabbing mine and Sammy's dishes, and Johnny went to stand. I shook my head at him, pointing my head to Joy.

He nodded, remaining in his seat.

After collecting the plates, I deposited them in the sink, washing my hands before moving to the cake. Cutting six slices, I slid them onto individual saucers and served them with dessert spoons to our guests.

By the time I took my seat, Logan's cake was practically gone. I laughed when I saw how much chocolate was on his cheeks.

I grinned, loving the way Johnny groaned when he tasted it. I slid the spoon into my mouth, licking the smudge of chocolate on the underside of the spoon as my eyes once again met Johnny's, just in time to see his mouth drop as he watched my tongue lick the spoon.

I wasn't a complete idiot. I had read enough cheesy romance novels to know that look.

I licked my bottom lip, watching his eyes widen and follow the movement. My breath stilted when I saw his hand lift from the top of the table and disappear beneath, and I was shocked when I saw him fidgeting.

I picked my saucer up, escaping to the kitchen.

What was wrong with me? I never got attracted to the opposite sex. Now I had to go and develop these stupid feelings for the campus stud.

I shook my head at myself, emptying the remains of my cake into the bin. I had suddenly lost my appetite. I turned around, surprised that I had company. Surprised and very thankful that it wasn't Johnny.

"Hi, Sammy." I smiled warmly at him, only now noticing how quiet he had been all night. "Let me take those."

He grinned, handing the plates over to me.

Standing at the sink, I dunked the plates beneath the water.

"How about you wash, and I dry?" He had a mischievous twinkle in his eye and his smile mirrored his brother's. How could I say no to that?

Whilst I was getting my fingers all wrinkly, Sammy described the mood of game day, and I laughed at his story-telling. Apparently, I was to prepare myself for the whole town to go crazy. Lots of people even wore face paint in the team's colors to cheer them on. He promised to get a hot dog with me at the game when I told him I had never been to one before. He was sweet, and I knew he'd make someone very happy.

I turned around after I'd washed the final spoon and saw Johnny standing in the doorway to the kitchen, watching mine and Sammy's interaction. He smiled shyly at me.

"You ready, bro?" he asked, looking past me at Sammy.

"Let me finish helping Tillie with these dishes and I'll be with you." He grinned, making use of one of Joy's cleanest towels on her rack, and seconds later, Johnny had joined in, helping Sammy to finish the dishes in double time.

Scooping healthy portions of both the spaghetti Bolognese and the lasagne into refillable tubs, I popped them in a plastic bag.

Walking into the lounge with Sammy and Johnny following me, I watched as Joy led Chunk and Logan to the front door. I smiled as I heard her chattering away to them.

Sammy gave me a small wave and walked on to the door.

"These are for you." I turned to Johnny, holding the bag out for him. "Thank you for tonight. Joy had a lovely time."

"You're welcome." He took the bag from me, our fingers gently grazing, and I gasped as a shiver shot up my arm, running down the length of my spine. My eyes remained locked with his, and I couldn't help but notice how his breathing had deepened in the same way mine had.

I pulled my hand back, not having a clue what that was—not wanting to know what it was.

He turned without saying a word and left. Not a smile. Not even bidding me good night. Just a quick kiss to Joy as he left.

My eyes filled with tears. Had I offended him or pissed him off?

I dragged my tired feet to the staircase, giving Joy a quick kiss to her cheek and ignoring the curious glance she gave me before making my way up the stairs.

Stripping off, I quickly slipped my strap top and shorts on, brushed my teeth and turned off the light, climbing into bed.

Sleep did not come easy. The whole night, I tossed and turned, my mind constantly replaying mine and Johnny's interaction. I was so confused by his reaction. I wasn't stupid; I knew he had been with dozens of girls, but I really didn't understand why I was the one to receive the brush off.

WAKING UP THE NEXT MORNING, his face was the first thing to flash through my mind before I had even opened my eyes. Rolling over, I grabbed my sketchpad off the floor and began drawing. Within moments, I had a pair of oval globes staring up at me from the page.

Climbing out of bed, I walked to the window, opening the curtains.

I froze on the spot.

Johnny was standing outside his house, staring up at my window. He was dressed in a pair of jogging bottoms, trainers and a white t-shirt.

I gave him a small wave, one that probably made me look like the most awkward person on this planet. After a few minutes, he gave me a small wave in return before turning around and walking into his house.

Feeling resigned, I allowed my eyes to trail up the wall of his house and then chuckled, surprised, when I saw Logan standing at his window—clothed, thankfully—waving at me like a loon. I laughed louder, waving back before going to get ready for my day out of the house. It looked like it was going to be a beautiful Saturday and I didn't plan to waste any of it.

SITTING down on one of the benches in the town square, watching all the people pass through, I scanned the crowds for my next subject. I always found it difficult to pick someone to draw; I needed someone kind of still, not all the shoppers hustling and bustling around. I blew out a breath when I realized this was really the wrong spot, and walking a few blocks, my eyes zeroed in on the coffee shop ahead on the corner. Ducking inside, I ordered myself a hot chocolate with marshmallows, cream and chocolate sprinkles. Anyone who didn't like this drink had to be crazy.

Taking my seat, I leaned back, warming my hands on my mug of chocolaty goodness.

Taking my pencil out, I focused on the elderly couple across from me and grinned. I loved the way the gentleman took the marshmallows from his saucer and added them to hers. It was clear they had been together a long time, and they were a perfect example of what we all wanted: someone to love us for eternity.

While I was absorbed in the detail on my sketch, I heard the chair across from me scrape, and frowning, I looked up, surprised when I saw it was Johnny taking a seat opposite me. I wanted to groan in frustration: he was kind of blocking my view of my couple and having him sitting so close to me was really going to mess with my nervous system.

"What are you doing here?" I asked, silently cringing at how rude I must have sounded.

"It's a free country." He looked so relaxed that I wanted to scream.

Was it all me? Had I fallen into a one-sided crush? Watching how cocky and self-assured he was, I was starting to believe that.

Peeking around him, I tried catching more detail and was determined to block out any distractions.

"You're avoiding me," he stated, cocking an eyebrow at me with a stupid grin on his face.

"I'm busy, as you can see." Putting pencil to paper again, I began shading in the lines of the gentleman's jacket, circling around the buttons.

Minutes later, Johnny sighed and left the table. I focused on my paper and not on the fact that he had left. Why should I care? It wasn't like we were friends or anything.

He returned with a fresh cup of hot chocolate for me, exactly as I'd originally ordered it. Only the new one had more chocolate sprinkles.

"Thank you." I smiled, taking a sip, licking the sprinkles from the cream.

He grinned, taking a copy of The Great Gatsby out of his bag, surprising me with his choice in literature.

I was putting the final touches on my sketch. Looking over, I smiled at the look on Johnny's face. He was resting his head on his left hand, his eyes trailing over the words. He had the cutest pout.

I chuckled, signing the bottom of the sketch before ripping it out.

"You finished?" he asked, closing his book.

I nodded, giving the sketch a last look. Before I could scrunch it up to discard it in the bin, Johnny quickly took it out of my hand and made his way across to the couple.

I was shocked and completely mortified that strangers would see my work—see that I had been staring at them for the last hour and a half, taking down all their intricate details.

Johnny turned, pointed at me and held the sketch to

the couple. The lady accepted it and gasped when she saw the sketch.

Just kill me now.

The couple gave me a small wave and I returned it but then directed my glare at Johnny.

He had no right to hand my sketch over to them. If I wanted someone to see my work, I'd give it to them myself. I fumed silently before standing and leaving the coffee house behind, Johnny included.

Unfortunately, he quickly caught up to me, grabbing my arm and spinning me around to face him. "Where are you speeding off to in a hurry?" He looked genuinely confused by my actions.

"You gave my sketch away to that couple!" I snapped, pointing behind him at the coffee house.

"That couple?" he asked incredulously, looking even more confused. "That couple," he replied, holding his hands up to do the speech mark symbol sarcastically, "were so touched by your drawing that the poor lady can't stop smiling."

"I don't care!" I snapped, sounding like a spoiled princess. "You had no right! I never wanted them to see it." I spun around, determined to get as far away from Johnny as I could, but I only managed to get a few steps away before his voice stopped me.

"It's their wedding anniversary. They said it was the perfect present to mark the occasion."

I froze on the spot, his words erasing the anger I had been feeling, replacing it with warmth.

He walked closer until I could feel him right behind me. "They said it meant the world to them."

I turned to him, smiling unconsciously. I couldn't help it. Knowing that the couple loved and appreciated what I had captured of them on paper erased all my negative feelings of self-doubt.

"There it is." He slowly reached up, cupping my face in his large palms. "There's my smile."

What the hell was he doing?

I pulled my head back. I didn't belong here, in this position with Johnny: an art geek and a football jock. I mentally rolled my eyes.

"Johnny..." I whispered, flicking my eyes down and back up, hoping he'd get the message.

He frowned, looking down at me, and then, shaking his head, he slowly let me go, stepping back from me.

"Go out with me," he whispered.

"What?" I laughed loudly. He must be crazy! Why the hell would I want to go out with someone who's only going to break me when he gets bored?

"Come on." He smirked down at me. "I'm not that horrible." His smile slowly faded. "Unless..." He cocked an eyebrow at me, waiting for me to fill in the blanks.

"Unless what?" I took the pencil out of his waiting hand, genuinely confused at whatever he was thinking, and tucking it inside my notepad, I turned my head to look at him.

"Unless it's Logan you'd really prefer standing in front of you?"

I'm sure he meant it as a statement, but it came out sounding like a question. This was the first time I had ever heard Johnny sound so doubtful. It made him seem more normal.

"I don't think of Logan like that." I shook my head.

"You sure?"

He didn't believe me. Obviously. He didn't know me. He just saw the outside shell. It was the middle he had to know to understand me, and that was my problem.

"I'm not right for you, Johnny." I gave him a tight smile, wanting to be out of this conversation. "I think we could work. I just don't think..." I sighed, getting flustered. "I don't think you're ready for the craziness that is me." I chuckled, trying to make light of the situation.

"I'll be the judge of that." He stepped toward me, his hands immediately latching onto my hips, pressing his tall frame against my short one. "Give me one chance. One. That's all I'm asking."

My eyes remained locked on his, watching for any sign. I liked to think I was a good judge of character and would be able to spot a lie if I saw one, but I was completely clueless when it came to Johnny.

"One chance." His fingers tensed against my jean-clad hips and desperation laced his tone.

"Can I think about it?"

He frowned, not happy with my reply.

"I'm taking a lot on here, Johnny." I stared at his chest, needing to be honest with him. "All the rumors going on about you." I shook my head, already feeling the icy chill of self-doubt grip me.

"No," he said coldly.

My eyes shot up to his, surprised at his words. No? Seriously? He was already trying to dictate shit to me?

"No thinking." He shook his head before a sexy smirk took over his face. "Let me take you out."

"Like a date?" I'm not going to lie. I was horrified at the thought. I was not a 'date' kind of person. Getting all dressed up and fancy for someone just wasn't my thing.

He shook his head, making me relax a little. "Come out with me tonight. Dressed as you are, if you want. Nothing fancy."

I narrowed my eyes at him, thinking over his suggestion. Dressed as I am? I suppose I could spare him an evening.

"One condition." I held up my index finger, giggling at the look of doubt on his face. "If it doesn't feel right, then that's it. Deal?" I held my pinkie finger up at him, giggling when he narrowed his eyes in a mock glare.

He lifted his hand, entwining his pinkie finger with mine. "Deal."

He leaned down, making me gasp.

Was he going to kiss me?

Dipping his head to the side, he pressed a soft kiss to my cheek. "I'll pick you up at 7pm." He grinned, slipping his hands into his trouser pockets.

I couldn't wipe the smile off my face, watching his ass as he walked away. Literally. He had the cutest butt. He turned his head, giving me a sexy wink, catching me staring after him.

I groaned in response, turning around and walking away.

I was so screwed.

IT WAS 18:55 and I was pacing the tile floor in Joy's

kitchen, sipping on my pint of milk. Drinking milk just always seemed to chill me out. Even when I was little.

"You okay, sweet girl?" Joy asked. She had a small smile on her face.

"I don't think I was this nervous when I'd told my father that I wanted to move away to go to college."

The doorbell rang, making me squeak in surprise.

"I wonder who that could be," Joy said, giving me a cheeky smile.

I rolled my eyes at her sarcasm. She knew exactly who it was, and I wouldn't have been surprised to find out she had organized all of this through a love spell or some crap. I had learned quickly that Joy was an old romantic, and me hooking up with her favorite guy would probably make her head explode. She went to the door, leaving me in the kitchen.

Looking down at myself, I had a moment of cockiness. I was dressed in my 'I am Groot' t-shirt, themed from the film Guardians of the Galaxy, and a pair of black jeans with worn away patches on the knees. Slipping my Ugg boots on, I was happy with my choice of clothes for the evening. This was me at the end of the day, and if Johnny couldn't handle that, then that said a lot about whether we could work.

Walking into the lounge, I laughed when I saw he was dressed in a pair of blue jeans and a white t-shirt with the words 'Return of the Chewbacca' on it. He grinned in response, his eyes doing a quick flick down to my chest and back up.

Joy rolled her eyes and held my coat out to me. "It's

cold out and you'll need it," she said with a cocked eyebrow.

I took the coat, slipped it on and wrapped my butterfly scarf around my neck.

"Any rules?" Johnny asked, directing the question to Joy. He was joking obviously, but Joy took it completely seriously.

"Home by eleven." She said it so seriously it made Johnny and I laugh, but she cocked an eyebrow, obviously not joking.

Johnny cleared his throat, looking serious. "She'll be back here by then." He gave Joy one of his charming smiles, disarming her on the spot and then holding his hand out and making me stare for a moment too long.

Joy fidgeted, softly clearing her throat and I rolled my eyes in response, stepping forward and taking his hand before we headed out of the house and made our way up the street toward campus.

"So," I replied, my fingers giving his a gentle squeeze. "Where are we going?"

"It's a surprise." He grinned down at me, giving me a cheeky wink. "If I told you, I'd have to kiss you."

I laughed at his unique spin on the overused line. Had to give him points for that.

He began leading me into a part of town I hadn't visited yet, making me wonder where the hell he was planning to take me.

"Are you lost?" I asked, worried that he was.

"What's with you and all the questions?" He laughed, looking down at me. "I've lived here for over a year. Don't you think I'd know my way around by now?"

I shrugged my shoulders, remaining silent. Obviously, he should've known where he was going, but the further we walked, the further away from people we seemed to get. The streets were getting quieter and every shop we seemed to pass now had their shutters down.

We turned a corner at the end of the block and I realized we were entering an industrial estate with workshops. Most were closed, but one up ahead was still open. It had all its lights still on and as Johnny led me around the side through to the back, I gasped when I realized where he had brought me.

We stopped walking and he positioned me in front of him, so I could see all the lights and equipment. I read the signs with my mouth dropping into one of the biggest grins ever: Rick's Paint Shack; an outdoor paintball range.

"So," he whispered in my ear, his lips licking the shell of my ear. "You ready to get all wet with me?"

I laughed at his completely filthy, sexual innuendo and turning to face him, I automatically threw my arms around his neck, hugging myself to him. "Absolutely." Taking his hand in mine, I began pulling him with me, excited to get started.

As we picked our team colors at the counter, I bounced on the spot.

"Excited?" He grinned down at me, his eyes twinkling with excitement.

I took my overalls from the lady at the counter, skipping off to the changing rooms. "Get ready to lose, Baker!"

DRESSED in pink overalls that were now covered in splotches of blue paint, my pink goggles firmly attached to my head, I hid behind a stack of hay, peeking over the top trying to find him. A few strands had come loose from my bun, which were also stained with paint, and I blew them off my face. Hearing movement to the side of me, I turned my head quickly, but before I could move, I was hit several times with more blue paint balls. I giggled, jumping to my feet and attempting to make a run for it when I was tackled from the side. I landed on my back with Johnny hovering over me.

"Give in yet?" He grinned down at me, knowing full well he had won this game.

I nodded, secretly loving the way he was looking at me—the way all girls wanted someone to look at them: like she was the only girl in the world.

"I really want to kiss you," he whispered, leaning his weight on his hands on either side of my head. "May I?"

I gasped, wanting him to do just that but too afraid to say. I slowly nodded, tilting my face a little toward his. He leaned down, pressing his lips softly to mine. They were so soft and gentle, which surprised me. Tilting his head to the side, he moved away, rubbing the tip of his nose against mine before pulling me to my feet.

We separated to remove our overalls and handed them back in. Johnny insisted on paying for the both of us, and moments later, we were making our way home. He held his hand out to me and I shyly accepted, entwining my fingers with his. We walked in silence, just our hands touching and my head resting against his upper arm—I wasn't tall enough to reach his shoulder comfortably. As we walked up our street, I sighed. The night had been perfect.

He walked me up the garden path, still not letting go of my hand.

"Thank you for tonight, Johnny." I smiled up at him, loving the way his grin stretched at my words.

"So, you had a good time, then?" he asked cockily.

"The best time." I blushed, looking down at our feet and groaned inwardly, frustrated with myself. Why couldn't I just be normal and look at him? He must have thought I was a complete freak.

He tucked his fingers beneath my chin, lifting my face to his.

"Will I see you tomorrow?" he asked, keeping my face tilted.

"I have classes tomorrow," I said, nodding. "I can meet you for lunch?"

He nodded, his lips slowly descending on mine, making my knees weak.

"Until tomorrow." He grinned, leaving me on my doorstep and making his way across the street.

I headed inside, where I was met by a waiting Joy who looked more excited than I did. I then spent the next hour washing all the paint out of my hair, excited for tomorrow to come.

6

JOHNNY

Tap. Tap. Tap. Tap.

I was repeatedly tapping my pencil against the table, not focusing on my accountancy essay in front of me. Every time that damn door would open, I'd get this stupid thrill of warmth shoot through me that it could be her.

I groaned in frustration, looking across the table. Logan sat there, leaning back in his chair, smirking his ass off at me.

"What?" I snapped, wanting to know what his problem was.

"Nothing." He chuckled. "Just wondering when Mr. Big Man on Campus turned into a girl."

Chunk laughed at his words, making me roll my eyes. If only they knew.

He frowned at me, fluffing the hair at the back of my head. "You've still got paint in your hair, man."

I shrugged him off. "Shut your trap, Charlie." I

emphasized his name, knowing how much he hated it. The paint was the least of my problems, even if it was bright pink. My eyes wandered back to the door again.

Where the hell was she? Had she changed her mind? Did she regret last night?

Maybe I shouldn't have kissed her. Fuck. I shouldn't have kissed her.

Looking back at the door, I saw there was a girl holding the door open, helping her friend carry some boxes. The door was just wide enough for me to see the large crowd forming outside. I quickly scanned the room, looking for Sammy.

Fuck, he wasn't there.

I shot up out of my seat, running to the door, hearing Chunk and Logan call my name.

He'd better not be in another fight.

Running out the door, I saw that the crowd was probably double the size of the last one. Pushing my way through, the space in front cleared in front of me, people turning to either gawk at me or whisper at me.

I got to the front, just in time to see Tillie push herself in between Sammy and the douche that wanted to rearrange his face. I kept calm long enough to see Tillie push him, looking up at him, attempting to look fierce. Instead she just looked like a scared kitten.

Before I could blink, the guy tried to push her out of the way. She retaliated by slapping him across the face. Damn, my girl could be fierce! The guy grabbed her, putting his hands on her hips. Which of course made me snap.

I marched forward, grabbing him by the scruff of his shirt, throwing him backwards. "Hands off!" I looked her over, making sure she wasn't hurt. "You okay?"

She nodded, turning to Sammy. She lifted her hand, assessing the damage on his lips before he shrugged her off and stormed past me.

"Hey! Sammy! Get back here!" I yelled after him.

Logan jogged after him, waving me off.

"I'm sorry about that," I apologized, picking Sammy's bag up off the floor. "He's not usually like that."

"That's okay." She reached over, stroking her fingers along the back of my hand.

I flipped it over, pulling her hand to my lips and pressed a kiss to her knuckles. "Thank you for sticking up for him."

"Don't worry about it." She leaned up on her tiptoes, pulling her hand from mine and wrapped her arms around my shoulders. "Do you think we should go and check on him?"

I shook my head negatively, resigned to let Logan deal with Sammy. He and I would be having words soon though.

"Sammy's been a little..." I shrugged my shoulders resigned. "Different. Since moving here." I shook my head, not liking the worry that came over her face.

"Then we should definitely go and check on him." She took my hand, leading me toward the path that Logan and Sammy disappeared down.

Walking home, I kept her hand in mine, liking the feel of it. The mood couldn't be ruined until she had to utter those words—the words I never really liked to hear coming from the female mouth, usually because they led to awkward conversations.

"So, after, can we talk?" she asked hesitantly, avoiding looking at me.

I tightened my hand on hers, swinging our arms between us slowly. "Sure." I looked down at her, trying to figure out what she was thinking.

Walking into the house, I let her hand go, jogging up the stairs to check if Sammy was there.

Nothing.

His quilt was still messy and there was no sign of him.

Going back down, I took a seat next to Tillie, not ready for this talk. "So, what did you want to talk about?" I reached for her hand, but she moved it away, tucking it beneath her leg.

"I... uh... I just wanted to say..." She swallowed, looking down at her lap. "That if you wanted to... you know... if you wanted to..."

I sighed, leaned over her and pulled her over to me. Sitting her so that she was straddling me, her eyes widened at the sudden change of position.

"That's better. Now..." I leaned back against the sofa, relaxing my back. "What were you trying to say?"

She placed her hand on my shoulders, supporting her weight so that she wasn't sitting on me.

"I don't think I can share you," she whispered, avoiding my eyes once again and staring at my chest.

I trailed my fingers up her sides before moving to her

arms. Taking her face in my palms, I pulled her head down to mine, our foreheads pressing together. "What makes you think I want anyone else?" I tilted my face, needing to feel her lips on mine. "If I'm with you, I'm with only you. Okay?"

She nodded, closing her eyes. That was the only signal I needed.

I pulled her head down to mine, our lips meeting softly.

Tillie was going to be the death of me.

Since moving here, I had basically had women on tap whenever I wanted. I had never had to go slow with one before. However, I knew every touch and memory with Tillie would be worth it.

I softly licked the seal of her lips, wanting her to open for me but not sure if she would. She tightened her fingers in the back of my hair causing my hips to unconsciously buck up against her.

She gasped as my hardness rubbed against her, but she didn't pull away, instead only held herself tighter to me.

I slowly slid my tongue in to press against hers, groaning at the sensation.

Fuck, she was amazing.

She wrapped her arms tighter around my shoulders, crushing her chest to mine. I fisted my hand in the back of her hair, loving how she felt in my arms. Pressing my tongue against hers, I tried to remember that this was probably a little fast for her, but I couldn't stop when I had her sexy body on mine.

She pulled her lips from mine, pulling her head away.

A beautiful blush stained her cheeks, traveling down to the column of her neck.

Fuck, did she blush all over when she was turned on?

"I'm sorry," she whispered. She gasped, her chest heaving right in front of me. "I shouldn't have done that." She shook her head, her palms resting on my shoulders. "I'm not ready for that."

I rubbed my hands up and down her sides, trying to comfort her. "It's okay," I whispered, trying to control the raging lust running through me.

She had no clue just how sexy she was. She quickly moved, choosing to sit next to me instead.

Watching her remove her jacket, I had to leave her for a few minutes.

Walking into the bathroom, I leaned my ass against the sink, trying to calm things down. Doing the two times table, I tried thinking of things to get rid of my problem. I couldn't sit next to her fully erect. She wasn't ready for my 'horny asshole' routine and to be with me intimately.

To be honest, I don't think I was even ready.

I had never had someone in my life that I wanted around for more than one night. She was perfect for me. Perfect to me. I didn't want to mess that up.

Walking back in the room, I saw she already had her pencil out and had begun twirling it in her hand. Taking my seat back beside her, I held my hand out, trying to show her that it was okay and hoping she would take it.

She smiled, entwining her hand with mine and

resting her shoulder on mine. Leaning my head against hers, I sighed happily.

Whoever thought I would be so soft with a girl?

She cuddled into me, heaving out a blissful sigh, content. Just like I was, hopefully.

My eyes shot open when a loud bang echoed from the doorway.

"Wake up, love birds," Chunk yelled, joining us on the sofa. He grinned down at Tillie, holding his hand out to her.

She gave him a shy smile, slipping her hand into his to shake it.

"Where's Sammy?" I asked, looking over Tillie's head.

Right then, the front door opened, and Sammy and Logan came in.

"Sit," I ordered, pointing to the chair opposite us. "Explain."

He sat, heaving out a deep breath. He looked at Tillie, giving her a small smile before his eyes settled on me. He looked exhausted and it made me want to smack him. This shit was not needed just a few weeks before the first game of the season.

"I may have laid some bets down on the other teams in my last year of high school."

"Are you fucking kidding me?" I yelled, directing my anger at Sammy. Tillie squeaked in surprise at my outburst. "Sorry," I apologized, hating that I was losing my shit in front of her. My eyes flickered to Logan stood behind him. "Did you know about this"

"He's not a child, dude," Logan defended.

"Obviously he is!" I paced in between them. This shit should not be happening. "You would be thrown off the team if the coach found out about this." My eyes shot to Chunk and I could see the look of disappointment on his face. I shook my head negatively. If Chunk weren't my best friend, Sammy would be completely screwed. "What does that have to do with you getting your ass kicked all the time?" I stared at him, waiting for a response.

I still didn't get an answer. He remained staring at the floor.

Before I could lose my last bit of patience, Tillie placed her hand on my arm, moving past me. She leaned down on her knees, right in front of Sammy. "Sammy," she whispered, rubbing his knee. "I know you and I don't know each other well, but I'd like to change that. Please talk to us. What happened?"

I smiled at her, trying to reach out to Sammy.

She was right, she didn't know him, but she wasn't letting that stop her. His eyes flicked up to hers, assessing her.

"We can't help you if we don't know what's going on," she said quietly, trying to make him comfortable and giving him another knee rub. "Come on, Sammy."

I loved her use of the word 'we'.

He held his hands out for hers and she immediately took them. This was going to be bad, especially if he needed to hold her hand.

"Just before graduation, Mom's health insurance increased." He was talking to me although his eyes remained fixed on Tillie. "It wasn't a problem, really, thanks to Dad's life insurance payments, but there was a cockup at the pharmacy. They said it would take thirty days before the insurance update reached them." His eyes flicked to mine and away in a few seconds. "She needed the pain killers." His eyes filled up, making me frustrated. "So, I took a bet from a few guys and I never paid them the money."

"Why didn't you come to me?" I snapped, frustrated at not only him but my mother as well. Before leaving, I had told her several times that if there were any problems to let me know and to not let Sammy get involved.

"Sammy, that was really brave of you," Tillie cooed at him.

I rolled my eyes. He had her wrapped around his little finger already.

"Johnny," she said, turning to me. "Do you..." Her gaze flicked to Sammy and then back to me. "Can you help him?" She turned her Bambi eyes on me, making me weak.

"Sure." I nodded my head. It was times like this I was thankful Dad had ensured to leave a life insurance policy behind for us.

"Why don't you go and pay those boys and I'll stay here with Sammy." She gave me a sweet smile.

I rolled my eyes, walking toward the main door.

"Yes, dear," I replied in a bored tone.

She giggled, bringing a smile to my face.

"I'll come with you," Chunk said, following me to the door. "I'll show you where they hang around."

HEADING TOWARD THE SPORTS GROUNDS, I rolled my eyes at their choice of location. They were obviously just hanging around, waiting until Sammy decided to show up. They'd be surprised.

"So, about these bets," Chunk said, starting the conversation that I was dreading. "How do you want to handle it?"

"I can't tell you what to do, man." I shook my head, frustrated. "You have to do what you feel is right."

"This could cost you everything," he snapped. "This last year you have played like a pro. You took a losing team and made them one of the top college teams."

I shook my head, not accepting the compliment. I did fuck all. We were a team at the end of the day. I just did my part.

"Just promise me it's over, bro. That's all I'm asking." He looked at me, a vulnerable expression on his face.

"It's over. I promise," I vowed to him. I was determined to keep that promise even if it killed me.

He held his fist out to me and I thumped it with mine. He nodded his head, signalling we were there.

Making a quick detour to the cash machine, I withdrew a few hundred. I had a feeling this little meetup was going to be expensive.

Arriving at the field, I walked ahead, sizing the boys up. They weren't a problem. Just little punks who thought they were bigger than they were. "Boys." I nodded my head in greeting. "I'm sure you know who I am."

A few nodded before one stepped forward, walking toward me and strutting from side to side with attitude.

"How much does he owe you?" I took my wallet out of my back pocket, ready to pay up. Sammy owed me big time.

"Five hundred," he replied with attitude.

I cocked an eyebrow at him, staring down at him.

He rolled his eyes, his shoulders slouching.

"Three hundred."

Handing the cash to him, I took note of the bruises on his knuckles. My hand tensed automatically, wanting to deliver every punch back at him. "No more beatings. We clear?" I threatened him.

He nodded, walking back to his friends. Hopefully that'd be the last of it.

"That wasn't so bad," Chunk commented, walking with me.

"So," he continued. "I noticed you and Tillie seem to be spending a lot of time together. Is that...?" He raised his eyebrows, expecting me to fill him in on any sordid details.

"Is that what?" I asked, wanting to know just what the hell he was trying to ask me.

"Come on, bro. Is she your fuck buddy for this weekend?" He raised his eyebrows mockingly, jiggling them up and down.

Any other time he asked me that, I would have just laughed it off, but not with Tillie. No fucking way. It was different. She was no fuck buddy—never would be if I had anything to say about it, which I did.

"She's different, man." I looked at him seriously,

hoping he'd try and understand. "She makes me feel... different. To all the rest."

He nodded, his face clearing of any sarcasm.

"That's cool, man."

We spent the rest of the walk home, chatting about the game. We were both ready for it but now we just wanted to spend the next few weeks getting the rest of the boys ready. If we could get to the championships, we'd be one happy team.

Walking to the house, I could see Joy peeking through her blinds, probably wondering where Tillie was. I gave her a small wave, seeing her smile and wave back to me.

Walking in, I laughed at the scene in front of me. Logan was flat on his back in the middle of the lounge room with his headphones on and Sammy and Tillie both sat on the sofa, challenging each other to a game of Need for Speed.

Chunk shut the door and Sammy immediately paused the game.

"Did it go okay?" he asked, nervously.

I nodded my head. "Don't let it happen again." I pointed at him. "It'll be more than a punch in the face next time."

I turned and walked into the kitchen, needing some space. Stress and I did not go well together. My eyes trailed to the door, thinking of my punching bag. My feet twitched. I could escape down there and release some tension.

My attention was quickly diverted when Tillie

entered the room. Before I could say anything, she walked straight up to me, wrapping her arms around my waist and resting her head on my chest. She squeezed herself to me and I wrapped my arms around her, gently rubbing her back.

"You are a good man, Johnny." She looked up at me, her eyes shining with unshed tears. "A really good man."

I leaned down, pressing my lips to hers. Humming against her taste, I wanted nothing more than to keep her here with me. I sighed, pulling away from her. "Joy was peeking through her window. I think she was worried about where you were." I frowned down at her, hating that we couldn't have had today to try to be normal

She sighed, looking as disappointed as I felt.

"Let me walk you home." I took her hand, leading her out of the house.

She waved to all the boys, leaving them to their arguments over the game.

Walking across the street, we both smiled when we saw Joy's window blinds twitch again.

"Sorry about today," I apologized when we reached her wall.

"Don't be." She smiled up at me, tightening her grasp on mine. "Today helped to fill in some blanks for me." She rested her head against my arm. "I feel like I know you more now."

"So, you're aware of how crazy my family is?" I joked, trying to make light of the situation.

She grinned, leaning up and pressing her lips to mine. "See you tomorrow."

Watching her walk up the garden path, my eyes immediately shot to her jean-clad ass. She turned her head, grinning when she saw where I was staring.

I chuckled, turning around and heading back home. A long, cold shower was needed.

7

———

TILLIE

WALKING FROM MY LIFE PORTRAIT CLASS, I GROANED in frustration. Of all the stupid projects he had to come up with, why did our professor have to come up with that! The assignment of the term was to draw a life portrait of someone in our lives.

Who the hell would agree to be my subject? Maybe I could ask Joy.

I was shaken out of my thoughts when someone collided with me from behind. I turned around, ready to unleash some anger on them when I heard Logan laughing. I rolled my eyes, not in the mood for him today.

"What's up, sugar?" He grinned, throwing his arm around my shoulders.

"Nothing." I shrugged him off.

If I survived this term, it'd be a miracle. Plus, I was a professional when it came to using pastels, but now I had to draw someone that would probably twitch every five seconds and use stupid shading pencils.

I followed Logan to the cafeteria, not feeling very sociable. Standing in the queue, I grabbed a ham sandwich and a pot of strawberries, paying the cashier and making my way to the table. I froze when an arm wrapped around my waist and a set of lips kissed the top of my head. I smiled, loving the way he was holding me.

"You smell delicious," he whispered.

I leaned my head back, smiling. As we walked forward with my back to his front, I noticed that a few people were stopping to turn and stare at us. Actually, it was more than a few. It was more like half the freaking cafeteria.

Taking our seats, I grinned at Logan. He was taking his tomatoes out of his sandwich and placing them on a napkin. He covered them by folding the napkin over them, and I frowned in confusion. Was he hiding his tomatoes?

Looking around, I could see people still staring and whispering. It was starting to freak me out.

"People are staring," I whispered, unwrapping the plastic from my sandwich.

Johnny tucked his index finger beneath my chin, turning my head in his direction.

"Ignore them." He leaned down and pressed his lips to mine softly, stopping all my worrying.

I smiled up at him, loving how open he was about... whatever we were.

Going back to my sandwich, I smiled at Sammy as he sat next to me. I laughed when I saw we had the exact same sandwich.

"Jinx!" we both said at the same time, making Johnny

laugh. He rolled his eyes mockingly before taking a bite of his pasta.

My eyes trailed across the room when I heard a high-pitched shriek of laughter. I froze when they settled on a group of cheerleaders. In the middle was Lucy Jones. She was the most popular girl around here.

She turned her head, no doubt feeling my stare. She glared at me before standing and making her way over to our table. I groaned, noticing the way she was walking like a duck: chest up and ass out.

"Hi, Johnny," she said in a fake cheery voice when she reached us.

"Hi, Lucy." He gave her a small smile and I didn't like it one bit. He shouldn't be smiling at her.

I rolled my eyes at myself. He could smile at whomever he wanted to smile at. It wasn't like we were exclusive or anything. He hadn't called me his girlfriend. I had no right to get jealous over him smiling at other girls. Right?

"So, are you ready for the game next week?" She twirled a piece of her long blond hair around her finger, giving a little giggle.

I turned away, instead choosing to look at Sammy. I couldn't keep looking at her. I didn't want to get my head kicked in for looking at her like she was an idiot, which she was.

"The team is ready," Johnny replied.

I rolled my eyes, making Sammy snicker. Did she think Johnny was Superman? That he played every position himself?

"Oh, yeah, of course."

Another giggle.

"So, what are you doing tonight?"

My eyes shot to hers. Was she serious? Did she not see the way he was holding me to him as we walked through the cafeteria?

"Training."

No smile this time. I mentally high fived myself.

"What about tomorrow?" she asked, leaning closer to him, her cleavage on full display. She smirked, obviously feeling in complete control and her hand slipped down to rest on his arm.

"I'm busy," he said sternly. His eyes quickly flicked to mine before reaching over and taking my hand in his. He brought it to his lips, pressing a kiss to my knuckles gently. "I'm busy every night," he said, looking back at Lucy.

Her eyes flashed with anger and hurt before they quickly disappeared. She leaned down so that her face was only a few centimetres from Johnny. "Let me know when you get bored." She smirked and walked away, swinging her hips from side to side.

She may have been talking to Johnny, but I knew who the message was really for. The worst thing was, she was right. He would get bored. I moved my arm, trying to pull my hand away. Instead, his fingers only tightened, not letting me escape.

"Let go," I whispered, not wanting to make a scene in the cafeteria, especially not in front of his brother and roommates.

He frowned down at me, looking genuinely confused.

"Johnny, let me go." I looked down at our hands, waiting for him to let go. He never did.

"Never," he whispered, rubbing his thumb over the top of my hand.

He was trying to soothe me, only Lucy's words kept repeating in my head. Plus, all the stares were just making me think that it was what everyone was thinking.

"I'm never letting go." He turned his body to mine and tilted his face in my direction. He tipped his head to mine and pressed his lips to mine softly. "It's just you and me. Okay?"

I slowly nodded, loving the sound of that.

"And me," Logan commented, giving me a lopsided grin.

"Me too." Sammy grinned at me, giving me a wink.

I laughed at them trying to include themselves.

Johnny rolled his eyes, closing the tub on his half-eaten pasta. "Weirdos."

Walking out of the cafeteria, I slung my backpack over my shoulder.

Logan slung his arm over my shoulders, walking with me. "So what class is next? I have boring massage therapy technique." He rolled his eyes.

"What are you studying to be?" I asked, confused. I thought he was a football player. Shouldn't he be studying something like management and finance? He'd need that to go with his career choice, surely.

"Sports therapy, my darling." He grinned down at me. "No way do I want to be stuck on a field for the rest of my life. I'm too damn good looking for that."

Johnny walked next to us, taking my other hand in his. "So, do I get you alone this afternoon?" He grinned down at me, making me blush.

"Uh, bro, you're kind of interrupting my time with Tillie." Logan cocked his eyebrow, seriously.

I laughed, shaking my head at him.

"You don't get time with Tillie, man." Johnny grinned, giving me a friendly wink before pulling me closer until I was no longer being hugged by Logan.

"Whatever." Logan laughed, his cocky nature in full force. "If I wanted Tillie, this round would already be over." Logan winked at me, letting me know he was teasing.

I couldn't lie. Logan was extremely good looking, but he was the guy that would break your heart. He didn't look like the 'settling down' type.

I was with the right guy. Or so I thought...

"Come and see me later." I leaned up and pressed a quick kiss to his cheek and jogged toward my building, where I spent the next three hours in a blissful state of landscape design.

LEAVING CLASS, I grinned at what was waiting outside for me. At the bottom of the steps, was a sight that was making most of the girls' stare. If it had been Lucy staring at him like that, I would have gotten green-eyed again, but I couldn't fault those that were staring. They had eyes. How could you not?

Walking down the stairs, I smiled at him. Johnny was sitting on the floor with his jacket to the side of him, with a pair of jeans, sneakers and a black t-shirt on. The shirt was a little tight and his muscly arms were on display.

Walking over to him, I smiled down, loving the way his eyes lit up when he looked at me.

"Don't you ever go to class?" I asked, jokingly.

He grinned, standing and wrapping his arm around my waist.

"Yes, sadly."

Walking home, my thoughts were running a million miles an hour. Would he help me? Or maybe he could help me in picking someone to draw? Maybe Joy could help me.

He groaned, looking frustrated. "What's wrong?" He frowned, looking confused. "You're really quiet."

I shook my head instantly. No way was I asking him to sit for me while I drew him. No. Way. As much as I wanted to, I just couldn't.

"Maybe I can help?" He shrugged his shoulders, trying to look optimistic. "Or at least help to look at it from another perspective?"

I nodded, agreeing. He kind of had a point. "I've been given an assignment to do by the second week of January." I was fidgeting with my hands against the strap of my backpack.

"Go on." He nodded, looking down at me.

"I have to draw a life portrait of someone." I bit my bottom lip, waiting for him to laugh or something.

"Why, Miss Jacobs, are you asking me to pose for

you?" he asked, sounding like Mr. Darcy from the Pride and Prejudice novel.

"No." I laughed, imagining him sitting there like a statue. He'd be fidgeting in minutes. "But I need to find someone."

"Seriously, draw me." He looked down at me. "It will give us an excuse to spend some time together."

"You're serious?" I asked, needing him to be completely clear.

"Yeah." He nodded, leaning down to plant a quick kiss on my lips. "I don't mind. Come over and we can start it today." He nodded his head toward his house, giving my hand a gentle pull.

"I can't." I shook my head, planting my feet firmly to the ground. "All my art stuff is here." I nodded my head upwards toward my bedroom window. "I have to demonstrate my art of shading and my pencil collection is up there."

"Okay," he said, not looking disappointed in the slightest. "I'll go and drop my stuff off and be with you in a few minutes."

I nodded my head, taking him at his word. "Come on up when you're ready," I said, walking away from him. "Joy is probably at her knitting club." I grinned, heading upstairs to my room.

On my door was a note from Joy saying she wouldn't be home until this evening.

Crap!

I hadn't thought this through. Now it was just going to be Johnny and me.

Alone.

In my bedroom.

I rolled my eyes at how horny my thoughts had suddenly become since this stupid crush had started.

Grabbing my sketchpad and still unopened strawberries from my bag, I threw them on my bed, not really having anywhere else to sit. Getting my pack of shading pencils that my father had gifted to me for my high school graduation, I began sharpening them, making sure they were all right.

"Knock, knock," Johnny called from my doorway.

"Come in." I waved him in, trying to keep things professional. "Grab that computer chair and move it to the centre of the room." I pointed at the chair.

He followed my instructions, taking a seat where I'd directed him to.

"Someone's being a little bossy." He winked, making me blush.

My heart sped up whenever he winked at me. Or smiled. Or talked to me. Fuck, I was so screwed. Hopefully Joy would come home earlier than planned.

"Would you like one?" I asked, holding the tub of strawberries to him.

He shook his head, making himself comfortable. "Would you like me to take my top off?" he asked, placing his hands on the hem of his t-shirt.

"No!" I practically yelled at him.

He smirked, obviously loving my reaction.

"Just sit there and relax."

He sighed, dropping his arms to his lap and doing just that. Relaxing.

I was ready to feel uncomfortable for the next hour. I

was prepared to have him stare at me constantly while I drew his frame, but he didn't. Instead, he split his time between watching me and looking around the room. His eyes routinely came back to the picture of my father and me at my graduation ceremony, but he never said anything.

I grabbed what was probably my fourth strawberry out of the tub and bit the bottom off it. I held it to my mouth, sucking some of the delicious juice from it. I sensed movement from the bottom of the bed and looked up, my eyes widening.

Johnny had stood up, the chair behind him seemingly forgotten.

"What are you doing?" I asked, surprised. Was he bored already? It hadn't been that long. I had only managed to get his upper body frame down. I still had so much detail to get.

His chest heaved, almost as though he had been jogging around the block, not sitting still in a chair. He moved toward the bottom of the bed and climbed onto it, moving swiftly up it until he got to me. He rolled up my pencil collection and gently placed it on the floor before taking my sketchpad off me and tossing it haphazardly to the floor with it.

He leaned over me, his knees on either side of my hips and pressed his lips swiftly to mine. He pulled back, his chest still heaving. "If you think I can sit there," he nodded his head behind him, cocking a sexy eyebrow at me, "while you eat those strawberries in the most erotic way I've ever seen, you are sorely mistaken."

That was all the warning I got.

He pressed his lips to mine, lowering me down so that my head was on my pillow. I wound my arms around his neck, parting my lips for him.

His tongue slowly entered, moving against mine.

It felt so good.

I unconsciously arched my back, rubbing my chest against his. I moaned softly, loving the way he felt against me. He groaned, his hands moving from either side of me to rest against my ribs. Seconds later, they slowly moved up until they were cupping my clothed breasts.

I gasped at the sensation, my head dropping back. His lips quickly descended, kissing and nipping down the column of my neck. He rotated the palms of his hands, squeezing my rather small cup size in his hands.

Fuck.

I was feeling things I had never felt before. If he could do this to me fully clothed, I was going to be totally screwed when the time came for us to see what's beneath the clothing.

Royally screwed.

Literally.

His hands trailed to the bottom of my shirt and began slowly lifting it up, his fingertips leaving electric sparks all over my skin.

I gasped, my hands going to the bottom of his shirt. I pulled it up and before I could get any further, he leaned back on his knees and began moving it up his body. He tossed it to the floor. My eyes trailed up, widening when I fully saw just how fit he was. I pulled my hands back. I froze, Lucy's voice flashing in my mind.

Shaking my head, I pushed him back so that I could

escape him. Walking to the door, I jumped in shock when Johnny ran ahead of me, slamming his hand against the door and shutting it.

"What happened?" he asked.

I ducked my head, not knowing how to explain.

How do you tell someone you're not good enough for them? I was never going to be a Lucy of the world. I was always just going to be me—my geeky, insecure self.

I wasn't stupid.

Johnny deserved someone who was confident and sexy and someone who knew what they wanted. Art was all I knew and letting someone in, offering myself up to love someone as much as I loved art, was scary and I was destined to fail at that.

I shook my head, crossing my arms across my chest.

"Don't shake your head." He took my head in his hands and tilted it until I was forced to look at him. "Stop pulling away from me." He sighed, staring into my eyes. "Is this because of Lucy?" He continued to look at me, waiting patiently for my answer.

I flicked my eyes away, feeling like a stupid, insecure girl.

He sighed, releasing his hold on me and taking my hand in his. He pulled me back toward the bed, only this time he sat on the side of the bed with his feet firmly planted to the floor. Positioning me in between his legs, he took hold of both of my hands and placed them on his shoulders before moving my right hand down until it rested over his heart.

Thump. Thump. Thump. Thump.

I smiled at the feel of his pulse beating through my hand.

"You feel that?" he asked, placing his hand over mine.

I nodded, blushing at the feel of his skin against mine. It was so soft. He had a light dusting of hair on his chest. Having my hand on his, a warmth began building in my chest. I slowly realized that warmth was a feeling. I had always felt skittish around the opposite sex, but right now, being here with Johnny, I felt completely safe. Protected.

"I will never hurt you," he whispered. "If I am with you, I am with only you."

He pressed a small kiss to my knuckles, my eyes closing.

I wanted to believe him so badly but there was still that part of me, a big part, that was scared to let go— scared to let him in fully.

I moved my eyes down to his, needing to trust him. "Have you ever slept with her?" I asked, needing him to be truthful.

"Never," he replied. "Nothing sexual has ever happened with Lucy."

I nodded, accepting his answer. "Okay."

He breathed out a sigh of relief at my answer. "Can we talk about the other problem?" He cocked an eyebrow at me, waiting for my reaction.

I frowned, confused. "Other problem?"

"Every time I touch you, when we're alone... when it goes past a certain line of intimacy, you freeze up."

Oh. That problem. "I, uh... I... well..." How the hell

did I explain this to a man that had slept with half of the college campus? "I'm a virgin."

His eyes widened in shock. "Well... okay. I wasn't expecting that answer." He chuckled, looking surprised. "So, you're all mine, then."

I blushed further at his words. 'Mine'. I'd be happy being his.

8

JOHNNY

Training was kicking my ass.

I had been sacked twice by my own teammate and threw the ball to the wrong side three times.

Fucking hell.

If I wasn't as good of a player as Coach knew I was, he would have benched me by now.

"Baker!" he yelled from the side of the field. "Get your head in the game!" He tapped his finger against the side of his head roughly.

"Dude, what's the problem?" Chunk asked, running next to me.

I shook my head. "No fucking clue. Things have just been tense, man."

"Well, knock that shit off." He frowned down at me before smirking. "I need my line-backer out there at the top of his game. Get her to rub one out or something." He nodded his head toward the stands that would be packed this weekend.

I stopped running.

Centred a few rows back, sat Tillie. She waved enthusiastically at me, grinning. I waved back, loving that she had chosen to come and watch us train. Well, 'watch' was a loose word. She had no clue about the rules of football. I had tried explaining them to her, but she quickly got bored and started talking about art pencils. She ducked her head, focusing back on her sketchpad. She never went anywhere without it.

The coach ordered the whole team to run suicides for the last twenty minutes of practice. It wasn't a problem for most of us as we were used to Coach's orders, but Sammy and Logan were struggling. Sweat was pouring off them and they were groaning like a couple of senior citizens.

The coach called time and it was followed by a few groans of enthusiasm. He smirked, walking toward his office.

I jogged over toward the bleachers as the rest of the team made their way to the changing rooms and I leaned over, giving Tillie a quick kiss. "What are you drawing?" I took a seat next to her and she immediately slung her legs over mine. I smiled at her growing confidence. Every day she was getting more comfortable around me.

She turned her sketchpad in my direction, grinning.

"Not bad." I shook my hand back and forth with an unimpressed expression. It was a beautiful and detailed sketch of the field we played on.

She rolled her eyes at me, scribbling her initials in the bottom right and dating it. I expected her to rip it out, but she never did. It stayed firmly attached to the spine.

"So, what are we doing?" She wrinkled her nose, her eyes flickering down to my chest before looking back up. "Aren't you going to shower?"

I laughed, tossing my head back. "What's the matter? I don't smell that bad." I slung my arm around her, pulling her toward me while digging my fingers into her ribs and tickling her.

"Stop! Stop tickling me!" she shrieked, trying to pull away from me.

I laughed, letting her move away.

One by one, each of the boys trickled out from the changing rooms and made their way to the exit of the field.

Logan and Sammy gave us a wave before jumping on their skateboards and escaping home. They had a 'Call of Duty' marathon that night with a few of the boys.

I stood up, holding my hands out to her. "Want to come in and wait for me while I take a shower?" I looked down at her, chuckling at the way her face blushed bright red before she took it.

Leading her into the locker room, I went to my locker, taking my towel and shower gel out before toeing off my shoes and socks. Winking at her, I walked between the lockers, taking my jersey off as I went.

The mirror ahead of me showed the way her eyes trailed over my back muscles before quickly looking away.

Standing beneath the spray, I zoned out, letting it run down my back muscles, soothing the burn there from practice.

After a few minutes, Tillie's voice filtered through.

"So, are you ready for the game next week?" It was higher pitched than normal but that was probably due to the ambience in there.

"I'm always ready." I wasn't being cocky. I was all ready for the game. My training, exercise and diet made sure that when it was game day, I wouldn't fail. Looking down, I groaned at the way my cock was standing at half-mast. It had basically been like that since I'd kissed her. It was used to having pussy on a regular basis and lately, it hadn't.

Grasping myself in my hands, I decided to rub one out.

No way could I fucking go out there fully erect. It would only scare her. Right now, I was on a mission to win her trust and acting like the horny jock was only going to push her away.

Pumping myself a few times, I groaned when her voice filtered back through.

"I can't wait to watch you win," she said excitedly.

Fuck, if she continued talking, I'd be marking this wall in no time. I closed my eyes, imagining what I had always stopped myself doing.: Tillie in my bed, her hair fanned out around her in a halo with my hand between her legs.

Fuck, she'd be perfect.

Completely untouched.

Only for me.

I groaned quietly, feeling my balls tighten at the vision of her in my bed: chest heaving, legs open for my touch, her hips slowly lifting off the bed, urging me to go deeper. Rougher. Harder.

I gasped, my eyes shooting open as I unloaded against the tile wall.

Fuck.

This girl was going to be the death of me.

"Everything okay?" she called. "You've gone really quiet."

Nothing got past her. I shook my head, chuckling. I directed the showerhead to wash my mess away before turning the shower off and wrapping the towel around my waist.

This was going to get interesting. In my rush to get in the shower, I'd left my clothes in my locker. Right where Tillie was sitting. Walking toward her, I smiled when I saw she was over by the picture cabinet. According to rumor, it was a cabinet of the previous teams the coach had trained. She had her face pressed so close to the glass, she was leaving little condensation marks when she breathed.

"What are you doing?" I asked, grabbing my underwear and jeans out of my locker.

"I'm just..." She froze, gawking at me before I slipped my left leg into my boxers followed by my jeans. She spun around so fast I thought she was going to collide with the glass.

I snickered. She really hadn't been expecting me to be standing behind her, practically naked. Lifting my jeans up, I kept the towel on until I could zip them up. Hoisting my Texas Cowboys t-shirt on, I walked toward her, wrapping my arms over her chest with her back to my front.

She leaned her head back against my chest, before pointing to the photo on the top shelf.

It was the oldest photo in the cabinet. It was of the coach's first team and it had been taken in the 1970's. It had been the first and last time the college had won the championships. We were determined to beat that record this year. Every member was determined to get to the championships and lift that cup.

She looked surprised that the coach had worked here so long.

She turned around and pressed a kiss to the column of my neck.

I swallowed heavily, not expecting her to do that. If she carried on, I'd be hard and ready to go for round two, which she really did not want to happen in the middle of the boys' locker room.

Grabbing my backpack, I led her out of the block and began walking her home. We spoke about our college essays mostly. I was trying hard to remember that art was her passion. I didn't want to fuck her first year up by taking up too much of her time. I'd keep her locked in my bedroom if I had my way.

Giving her a kiss, I kept it PG and watched her go inside.

It was pitch black when I walked into the house and flicking the light on, I headed upstairs, determined to get some research done for my Economics class the next day. Walking into my room, I froze in the doorway. There, on my bed, was a half-naked female student and sadly, not just any female student...

Lucy Fucking Jones.

She was dressed in pink, lacy lingerie lying on her stomach with her legs at the foot of my bed.

I walked toward her, causing the smile on her face to grow. As I reached her, her hand automatically went out, catching hold of the buckle on my waist. She had lust in her eyes and she assumed I was going to deliver.

No fucking chance.

"Get the fuck out of my bed!" I snapped.

Her eyes widened in shock at my outburst. "Excuse me?" she shrieked. Sitting on her knees, she put her hands on her hips, looking at me in shock. "I know you want me!"

My eyes trailed down to her chest, noticing the way her tits were pushed together and forming a very edible cleavage. If she were Tillie, I'd already be on her, but she wasn't.

"You heard me!" I grabbed her clothes neatly folded off my desk and tossed them at her. "Go and seduce some other idiot."

Her eyes filled with tears, but I just didn't have it in me to care. Not with her.

She slammed my door as she left, stomping down the stairs.

I rolled my eyes, taking the seat at my desk and turned the laptop on.

It was time to lose myself in the boring world of political statistics.

JOGGING TO CAMPUS, I cringed when I realized I

was twenty minutes late for my first class. Falling asleep at my desk last night hadn't been part of the plan. Running inside the marketing building, I snuck through the door when the professor's back was turned.

Taking my seat, I wanted to high five myself when it went unnoticed. Grabbing my note pad, I cringed when the professor turned around, his eyes immediately settling on me.

"Thank you for joining us, Mr. Baker." He cocked his eyebrow at me, making me feel about two feet tall.

I smiled politely, giving him a two-fingered army salute. He rolled his eyes, turning back to the board.

I grabbed my pen, taking down as many notes off the board as I could. One thing I hated about this class was that he used a lot of algorithms. I had enough trouble remembering shit without him throwing those in.

My phone vibrated in my pocket, disturbing me. I ignored it until the class was over. Forty minutes later, it vibrated a few more times. The professor called the end of the class with orders to catch up on the handout. Tossing everything in my bag, I exited class, taking my phone out of my pocket. I had several text messages of congratulations from a few boys off the team.

What the hell was going on?

I then got to a few messages off Logan asking me what the fuck I was playing at?

I replied, asking him what the fuck his problem was.

I froze when I got a reply.

They say a picture can say a thousand words. This one did. It was a picture of me in my room from last night—more importantly, a picture of Lucy and me with her hand on my belt buckle. He sent more pictures of Lucy on my bed. Some were censored but a lot weren't.

I was going to fucking kill her.

Turning around, I ran straight into her.

"Hello, lover." She slid her arm around my neck, attempting to pull me toward her.

"What the fuck have you done?" I'd never wanted to hit a woman as much as I did right then.

"Sweet, little Tillie isn't going to want you now." She smiled up at me before walking away.

Fuck. Tillie.

I ran down the corridor and didn't stop until I reached the art building. Spotting Bex in the crowd, I ran up to her. She'd know where Tillie was.

"Where is she?" I gasped, my chest tight with lack of breath.

She turned, narrowing her eyes and her lip curling at me in disgust. "She never showed up." Her eyes flickered down and back up. "Not that I'm surprised."

"I didn't cheat on her," I replied, trying to reason with her. "I would never do that to her." I swallowed, trying not to let the anger coursing through me get me into any more trouble. "I'm crazy about her, Bex."

"Whatever." She walked past me, obviously refusing to help me. "If you want to see her, you should know where she is." She walked into the building, leaving me.

I turned around, heading straight home. Knocking on Joy's door, I waited for an answer. I didn't want to just walk straight in like I normally would, if she was pissed at me.

Joy answered the door, smiling up at me. "Johnny! Is everything okay?"

She looked far too happy to see me if Tillie had seen those photos. She should be ready to hit me.

"Is Tillie here?" I frowned, completely screwed. If Tillie wasn't there, then where the hell would she go?

"No." Joy frowned, worry creasing her eyes. "She should be at school."

I nodded, trying to think of an easy lie I could pass off as the truth. "She probably is. I thought she said she had a free lesson, but I must have misheard her." I grinned, trying to look relaxed.

She smiled, nodding. "I'll tell her you stopped by."

I nodded, turning around and leaving. Stopping outside her house, I looked up and down the street. Turning left, I headed away from campus, determined to find her.

Walking several blocks, I looked up and down every side street and every shop window. She was nowhere in sight. Jogging across the street, I spotted the skate park that Sammy liked to hang out at. Walking through the gate, I spotted Sammy sitting by a large oak tree. He got up and jogged across to me.

"Have you seen Tillie?" I asked, desperation in my tone.

"Dude, what happened?" He looked stressed. I wasn't sure if it was for me or because of me. "How could you do that to Tillie?"

"I didn't!" I yelled.

His eyes widened at my tone and he took a step back.

I sighed, taking a deep breath. Trying not to take my unused anger out on him.

"After training last night, I walked Tillie home. I then walked inside the house, went upstairs and that's where I found Lucy. That's when I tossed her out of my bed and threw her out of the house." I sighed, looking down. "I've lost her, man." I had never been this hung up on a girl before. Tillie had quickly become everything to me. I wasn't ready for this to be over.

Sammy looked behind him and nodded, which confused the hell out of me. He stepped aside and there she was. She was so tiny that she could hide behind Sammy perfectly.

"Tillie..." I was shocked. She was there. I looked at Sammy and he gave me a small smile.

"I'll leave you guys alone." He looked down at Tillie, who gave him a small nod.

"Thank you, Sammy." She took hold of his hand, squeezing gently before letting go.

He nodded, giving me a comforting pat on the shoulder before leaving us alone.

I took a step forward, wanting to hold her.

She responded by taking a step away from me. She looked scared.

I could handle scared, but I couldn't handle her looking at me like I was the monster beneath her bed. Her cheeks were red and blotchy. She had been crying. She fiddled with the ends of her sleeves, pulling them down until they were basically covering her hands.

"Did you mean what you said to Sammy?" she asked,

whispering. Her eyes rose to meet mine. "Or were you lying?" Her eyes slowly filled with unshed tears.

"I wasn't lying." I shook my head, at a loss of what to say. "I promise. Nothing happened." I stared down at her, needing her to believe me. Walking away from here without her wasn't an option. She was leaving with me. There was no other way. "Lucy is a bitch and will always be a bitch. She wants me. I don't want her." I stepped forward until I was closer. Taking her face in my hands, I quickly rubbed away the few tears that leaked from her beautiful Bambi eyes with my thumbs. "The girl I want is here. Right in front of me. No other."

She shook her head, stepping away from me. "I don't believe you," she whispered. "You hurt me, Johnny."

I growled, stepping forward and pinning her against the tree behind her.

She squeaked in surprise, shocked at my actions.

I slid my hands down her back until I could grasp her ass cheeks and hoisted her up. My hands trailed down to the back of her thighs and wrapped them around my waist. I turned her head up toward me and slammed my lips down on hers. She gasped, allowing me to thrust my tongue inside to dance with hers. I pressed against her, feeling her breasts against my chest.

I groaned, kissing her rougher. I always tried to be calm and gentle with Tillie, but she was fucking frying my nerves. I know I made shit look easy but being with her—and only her—wasn't fucking easy. No women meant I was frustrated all the fucking time. My punch bag had been taking most of the tension coursing through my body. If she thought I was going to walk away and leave her, she obviously didn't know me very fucking well.

I groaned, rocking my hips against hers. The feel of her luscious body against mine was making me as hard as a rock. My cock was doing a happy dance at the thought of doing anything sexual with Tillie. I pulled my lips away from hers.

"Do you feel that?" I rocked my hips against her, once more. I groaned at how warm she felt between her legs. "Feel it?" I asked.

She gasped, nodding her head like an enthusiastic kid at a candy store. Her lips were red and swollen from the force of our kiss.

"That's for you," I whispered. I dropped my head, resting my forehead against hers. "I promise, Tillie. I have never and will never be unfaithful to you. I am with you and only you."

"I'm not ready to be..." she closed her eyes, taking a deep breath before opening them again. "I'm not ready to have sex with you."

"Then we'll wait," I whispered. I rubbed my nose against hers, making her smile a little. "I'm yours, whether it involves sex or not. When you're ready, I'll be here."

Her fingers entwined in the curls at the back of my head. "Promise?" she asked, looking vulnerable. She had hope in her voice, but she still looked scared.

"I promise."

She nodded, bringing her lips back to mine.

9

TILLIE

Resting my head against the tree behind me, I ran my fingers up and down the column of his neck. He looked like he was telling the truth. He turned his head and pressed a kiss against my wrist. Tingles shot up my arm, making me shiver.

"Will you come home with me?" He asked, tucking some loose strands behind my ears. "Maybe we can talk some more?"

I nodded my head. "That would be nice."

He unwrapped my legs, lowering me to the ground. Taking my hand, we silently walked back to his house and headed up to his room. He sat me on the bed before sliding his computer chair over and sitting opposite me. He parted his legs, putting them on either side of mine and taking my hands, resting them on my thighs.

"Can we talk about something else?" He looked at me cautiously.

I frowned, wondering what he would have to be cautious about. I nodded, trying to give him a smile.

"Can I ask..." He straightened up, looking uncomfortable before taking a deep breath. "Is there a reason why you pull away from me? Sexually?"

With that one word, I froze. I tucked my knees up on the bed and shimmied back so that I was leaning against his headboard.

He frowned at me, probably thinking I was putting distance between us but I wasn't. I just needed...

Fuck, he was right.

I needed some distance if he wanted to have this conversation now.

"When I was fourteen, I got into a little trouble." I stared at his doorway, not able to handle looking at him at the same time. "I was out with some friends and my mom was supposed to pick me up, like she did every night." I smiled at the memory of her, still missing her vanilla scent. I shook my head, trying to clear it. "Anyway, one night she never came. I was waiting and there was still no sign of her." My eyes watered and I quickly wiped them, determined not to get emotional. "A police car with flashing lights pulled up and took me home. I asked where my mom was, and they told me that my father would explain when I got home."

Johnny leaned over, taking hold of my hand. I entwined my fingers with his, appreciating the comfort he was offering me.

"I got home, and my mom wasn't there. My dad explained to me that she had left home at the normal time but..." I was trying to stay calm—to recite the facts to

Johnny the best way I could—but, I couldn't. She was my mom and she was more than just a fact. "She had been raped and beaten. Her car had broken down and she was walking to meet me." I held my breath, trying to keep the building sob in. I didn't want to break down in front of Johnny. "She had several knife wounds and died before the ambulance arrived." I sobbed, holding my hand over my mouth to try and keep the noise at a minimum. It didn't work, however. Seconds later, I was sobbing into my knees like a pathetic, dramatic mess.

I felt Johnny move toward me and pick me up. He sat on the end of the bed, placing me on his lap. I didn't hesitate in wrapping my arms around his neck and sobbed into his chest. I expected him to push me away when I told him about my mother's death, or just leave me alone. He never did. He rocked me gently, rubbing my back soothingly and pressing soft kisses to the top of my head.

I don't know how long I stayed sitting on his lap, cuddled in his strong arms with my head resting on his chest. I looked at his shirt, rubbing the wet patch I had left on it.

"You have ruined my shirt," he joked, looking down at where I was rubbing.

I giggled, resting my head back in its place on his chest.

"So," he started, sounding nervous. "That's why you're afraid to be intimate with me."

I nodded. "Ever since then, I've been skittish around boys. I'm good at being friends with them but sex..." I blew out a deep breath, "It scares me."

"That's understandable, Till." He pressed another

kiss to my forehead. "But you know I won't hurt you. Right?"

I hated that he sounded so unsure. I hated that I was widening the crater that was between us, but I just couldn't be like Lucy. I don't think I could ever be as sexually confident as she appeared to be. I nodded, pulling my head away to look up at him. "I'm sorry."

"You know I would never hurt you like that?" he asked. He had a look of warmth on his face.

I basked in it. I knew he would never hurt me. Trusting he would never hurt me was a different question, though. "I do." I frowned, staring at his collarbones. "I just need to move slower than..."

"Than Lucy?" he asked, cocking his eyebrow at me.

I nodded. At least he knew what was making my insecurities worse.

"Just promise me, that if the time comes where you don't want me—where you'd be happier with someone like Lucy—just tell me." I threaded my fingers into the back of his hair, massaging his scalp. "Don't string me along."

He smirked, leaning his face closer to mine before standing abruptly, taking me with him and making me shriek. He turned around and dropped me on the bed, unceremoniously.

I giggled, bouncing a few times on the springs before he lay down next to me. He grinned, leaning his head down and moulding his lips to mine. I parted my lips, moving my tongue against his. I hummed at his taste, holding myself against him.

He pulled away, smiling down at me. "Does that feel

like I would prefer to be with that brainless bimbo?" He cocked his eyebrow at me.

I shook my head, allowing him to pull me toward him. My head settled on his chest, feeling the pulse of his heartbeat through his chest. I sighed, feeling lighter than I had done in a long time.

I must have dozed off because when I opened my eyes, we were still in our spots, but Johnny was holding a piece of paper in his hands, his eyes flicking over it.

"What's that?" I whispered.

He smiled, dropping the paper on the floor, wrapping me in both of his arms. "Just some presentation pointers." He smiled down at me. "I have to go and get ready for practice."

I nodded, letting him go. He grabbed his bag and held his hand out for mine. I gave him a quick kiss before walking over to Joy's. I took a seat next to her, laying my head in her lap. She slid her fingers into my hair and began smoothing my hair down. I closed my eyes, feeling relaxed.

"That feels nice," I whispered. My mother used to do it when I was a little girl. I remember it used to relax me so much, I'd usually end up falling asleep.

"Johnny was here earlier," she said. "Did he find you?"

I nodded, staring at the wall on the floor.

"Is everything okay, my sweet?"

I smiled, tearing up at her nickname for me.

"You didn't seem very happy before you left for school."

"I wasn't." I sat up, crossing my legs and facing her.

"Johnny has a few... issues." I opened my mouth to tell her more when the doorbell rang. I groaned, going to answer it.

"Bex!" I was surprised she was there. "Come in."

She stepped over the threshold, walking straight past me and going in to the lounge. I chuckled when she took my spot next to Joy, grinning at me.

"Make yourself at home," I mocked, taking a seat in the armchair.

She laughed, kicking her shoes off and tucking her legs beneath her ass.

"I'm Bex." She held her hand out to Joy. "I'm Tillie's bestie from school."

"I like you." Joy wrapped her arm around Bex, both laughing at the action.

"Johnny was looking for you," Bex said, turning her head in my direction. "Did you guys have a chance to talk about the Lucy drama?"

I widened my eyes at her. I really did not want to have this conversation in front of Joy. Joy's head flickered between Bex and me before Bex gave in and rolled her eyes.

She dug through her bag and grinned, pulling a bottle of wine out with a cheeky glint in her eye.

"I'll get the glasses," Joy chuckled, getting up and walking to the kitchen.

"What are you doing?" I widened my eyes at Bex, waiting for her to get the message.

"What?" She rolled her eyes at me. "I'm dying to know the goss."

"Yeah but..." I stopped talking when Joy shuffled

back into the room.

"Now, fill me in ladies." She set the glasses on the table, taking the bottle off Bex and popping the cork. "What has that boy done?"

I laughed at her no-nonsense tone. I shuffled on my bum so that I was closer to the coffee table. Picking my glass up, I raised it and waited for them to clink their glasses to mine. Taking a sip, I hummed at how fruity it was.

"So, fill us in. What did the idiot do?" Bex asked, cocking an eyebrow at me.

I rolled my eyes in response. The girl would not shut up. "Basically," I said, my eyes turning to Joy, "pictures were plastered all over social media and in text messages of Lucy and Johnny together in his room last night."

"Oh dear." She had a disappointed look on her face.

"But..." I interjected, my eyes going to Bex. "It wasn't true. She was in his room, but he threw her out." I shrugged my shoulders.

"Do you believe him?" Bex asked, cocking an eyebrow at me.

"Yes." I nodded my head. "I trust him. I think."

Bex shrugged her shoulders dismissively.

"Who's Lucy?" Joy asked.

"She's a cheerleader bitch who thinks she owns the college. She probably thinks the most popular girl should obviously be with the most popular guy." Bex rolled her eyes in disgust.

"He's a good boy, though," Joy interjected. "He's a good one, especially to that brother of his."

I smiled at the look of adoration she always wore on

her face when talking about those boys.

A COUPLE OF HOURS LATER, I was lying on my back, laughing at the Simpsons impressions Bex was doing. This girl was a pro. She obviously loved the Simpsons a bit too much. She could do Ned Flanders perfectly, even when tipsy.

I turned to the side and grabbed my phone: six missed calls—all from Johnny.

There was a knock on the door and Joy quickly went to answer it, leaving me laughing at Bex's Mr. Burns impression. She was going to make her future mister crazy.

"Hello, boys," Joy greeted her visitors. "She's right in there."

I grinned when Johnny crossed her threshold, his eyes landing right on me. He was followed by Logan, who was wrapped in his coat and scarf and rubbing his hands together to ward off the chill. His eyes went to the three empty wine bottles on the coffee table before back to me with a smirk on his face.

Holy crap! When did we get through those? No wonder I was feeling all giggly.

"Hey, you." Johnny stood over me, smiling down at me. "We had too much to drink?"

I shook my head, looking up at him. He leaned down, taking my hands in his and pulling me to my feet.

"I'm going to take off," Bex said, getting to her feet, too. "Why don't you let lover boy tuck you in?" She waggled her eyebrows mockingly. "And you," she pointed at Logan, "can walk my drunken ass home."

"After you, darling." He gave me a cheeky wink before following Bex out of the door.

"Mind if I take her up?" Johnny asked, directing his question to Joy. He picked me up in his arms, walking past Joy.

"Of course not, sweet boy." She stepped aside, watching him carry me up the stairs.

I waved at her, only now realizing how many glasses I'd had when I saw dual figures of Joy standing there. As we walked through my door, I tightened my arms around his neck. He leaned down, placing me on my bed.

I kept my arms around his shoulders, refusing to let go.

"I'll see you in the morning." He pressed his lips to mine in what I assumed was supposed to be only a short kiss.

"Don't go yet." I squeezed myself to him, not wanting to let go. I don't know whether the alcohol was giving me more confidence or whether it was just me being open to feeling more. "Close the door," I whispered against his lips.

"Joy is right downstairs," he whispered, his eyes flicking to the doorway. "It's late."

"Not that late," I whispered. I leaned up, pressing a kiss to his neck. "Stay." I peeked my tongue out, sucking gently against his pulse point. "Just for a few minutes."

He sighed, getting up and walking toward the door. He looked back at me, nibbling his bottom lip. He looked conflicted. Maybe he thought he would be taking advantage, but I wasn't that drunk. He shut the door and walked back over to me. He joined me back on the bed, lying at my side.

"Kiss me," I whispered.

He leaned down, pressing his lips to mine. I gasped, parting my lips. He pressed himself closer to me. I pulled his shoulders so that he was closer but ended up with him choosing to lie over me. His palms traveled down over my ribs until he was cupping the cheeks of my ass.

I gasped, thrusting my chest out, causing him to groan at the contact. His hands slid down to the back of my thighs and pulled them up and wrapped them around his hips. I moaned at the closer contact, tearing my lips from his.

Fuck, I never knew I could feel like this.

I moaned, thrusting my hips against his gently. He groaned, dropping his head into my neck.

"Fuck, Tillie." He pressed his lips back to mine before getting up and leaving me on the bed. "I will see you tomorrow." He walked out, leaving me a quivering mess.

I got up, stripping out of my clothes and into my comfy pyjamas. Climbing back in, I rolled over when my phone lit up with a text message from Johnny.

Sleep tight. It killed me to leave. If Joy hadn't been downstairs…

I giggled at the threat. Locking my phone, I placed it on the bedside table, dozing off in minutes.

WALKING to school the following morning, I cringed at the sunlight. Wine was the enemy. I saw Bex up ahead sitting on a wall with her sketchpad. Scrap that. Bex with wine was the enemy.

"Morning, sunshine," she called to me, making me cringe. "Ooh, not doing so well this morning."

"No." I frowned at her, with a sulky pissed off expression on my face. "Because of you and your wine, I basically threw myself at Johnny last night."

She tossed her head back, laughing. "And he turned you down? Damn, I'm liking him more and more every day."

"So, what happened with Logan?" I asked, wiggling my eyebrows at her, mockingly. Taking my mini bottle of orange juice out of my bag, I twisted the cap, taking a sip.

She rolled her eyes at my dramatics. "Ugh, nothing." She smirked before continuing. "If I swung that way, though, I'd be all over him."

I spat the orange juice out of my mouth, narrowly missing her leg. I was shocked. She was a lesbian? How did I not know this? "I'm sorry." I chuckled awkwardly, already feeling the blush creep up my neck. "I, uh, didn't know that you were a..."

"A lesbian?" She cocked her eyebrow at me, still grinning. She obviously wasn't offended by my reaction. "I thought you knew," she said, looking confused.

"Uh, no." I shook my head, wanting nothing more than to be out of this conversation.

"Seriously? Girl, you need to pay attention to what's

happening around you."

I chuckled, nodding my head in agreement with her. I shrieked when a set of hands landed on my ribs and dug their fingers into my ticklish spots. I slung my arm out to grab them before Logan quickly jumped away.

Johnny's arms slowly wound around me, pressing a kiss to my cheek. "Good morning," he whispered, nuzzling my neck. "Can I walk you to class?"

I nodded, taking his hand in mine and leading him to my building, leaving Logan and Bex laughing at something on her sketchpad. Sammy skated past us, giving me a small salute before disappearing into the crowd.

We walked in silence before I snapped under the pressure. "I'm sorry about last night!" I apologized, peeking up at him. "I'm not normally like that. I didn't mean to push—"

"Shhh!" Johnny said, pulling me to a stop and pressing his finger against my lips. "I'm not complaining." He grinned down at me before his eyes trailed down my body and then back up. "I liked you showing that part of yourself to me."

"You did?" I asked, surprised.

"Yeah." He slipped his hands into my back pockets and pulled me toward him. "It's nice to know you want me as much as I want you."

"I do." I smiled, wrapping my arms around his shoulders. "I'm happy with you."

His grin widened before he leaned his head down and pressed his lips chastely to mine.

"I have to go." I pulled away from him, giving him a small wave. "Come and see me later."

10

JOHNNY

Running down the field, I held my arms up, ready to receive the ball Chunk had just thrown. I caught it and ran the last ten yards, getting a clean touchdown. The coach did a mid-air fist bump, which was usually his signal that he was impressed. Sammy and Logan fist bumped each other on the bench and Chunk grabbed me in a headlock, making me laugh. Standing back up, my eyes went to the stands where Tillie was. I expected to see her clapping or smiling. Doing something at least. Instead she was sitting there, head down, sketching.

I chuckled, following the boys into the locker room. After a quick shower and change, I was back out, jogging over to Tillie, where she met me at the bottom of the bleachers.

"Where are we going?" she asked, slinging her backpack onto her back.

"Well, I was going to ask if you wanted to come back to the house?"

Her doe-like eyes flicked up to mine before I continued.

"Just the two of us."

I knew what I was asking her may be difficult for her. I didn't want it to push her away from me. After leaving her last night, I couldn't switch off. I was hard as a rock, but no way could I dry hump her with Joy downstairs. Plus, Tillie had obviously had one too many drinks.

"Okay." She nodded, resting her weight against my shoulder and her head against my upper arm. She stayed like that the whole way home.

She slid her bag off and dropped it by the wall. Walking inside, I took my coat off and draped it over the sofa. Looking over my shoulder, I saw her take a few steps up the stairs. She turned and held her hand out to me, looking as sexy as hell.

"Can we go upstairs?" she asked, vulnerability present in her tone.

I walked toward her, taking her hand and following her up. She had to take the lead in this.

Walking into my room, she turned toward me and placed her hands on my shoulders. With one short jump, she wrapped her arms and legs around me. "Don't break me," she whispered. She threaded her fingers through the back of my hair.

"I won't." I stepped forward, laying her down on my bed. Climbing over her, I lay next to her, not wanting to crowd her space too much. Before I could blink, she climbed over me, her hands and knees on either side of me.

I leaned my head up, pressing my lips to hers. She

smiled before kissing me back, parting her lips. I entwined my tongue to tangle with hers, closing my eyes at the sensation. I was proud of her for being comfortable enough to position herself over me. After a few moments, though, I could feel her muscles beginning to tense.

I held her toward me and rolled us over, being careful not to crush her with my weight. She bent her legs, parting them wider. I trailed my lips down to her neck and began nibbling softly on her beautiful skin. She gasped, her hips rotating at the sensation. As she did that, she rubbed herself against me.

I groaned at the sensation, feeling how soft and warm she was.

She let out a small noise at the contact, her hands tightening on my shoulder blades.

"Do I feel okay?" she asked.

It was such an innocent question, but it went straight to my cock. I felt myself harden further, rubbing against her more. "You feel amazing." I kissed behind her ear, loving the half-gasp, half-moan that came from her. I moved against her harder, causing her to curve her spine. "Does it feel good?" I asked, rotating my hips against hers.

She nodded her head, holding herself tighter to me and crushing her legs tighter against my hips.

She looked fucking amazing beneath me.

Knowing that I was the only one that had been like this with her wasn't helping my stiff cock from rubbing against her. My mind was stuck on a constant loop of how she would feel. How she would sound on the edge of pleasure. Would she be a gentle moaner or lose all caution and be a screamer when I was inside her?

I rocked against her harder, knowing full well I was losing myself to my thoughts, but I couldn't help it. I wanted her to come undone. No. I *needed* her to come undone. She had ruined me for any other girl and I wanted to be the same for her.

She gasped, her head thrown back and her neck exposed. I leaned down, my chest moving against hers. I rotated my hips, feeling the warmth from between her legs getting hotter.

Fuck.

I could imagine how wet she would be. I couldn't wait for her to be comfortable enough with me so that I could feel it for myself.

"I, uh..." She gasped, pressing her lips to mine. She dug her teeth onto my bottom lip, pulling it into her mouth before soothing it with her tongue. She opened her beautiful brown eyes and stared into mine. "I feel..."

"Yes, baby." I rocked my hips harder, more forcefully, needing to see her come apart in my arms. I wondered if this was going to be her first orgasm—the first of many if I had any say in it. "Let go. I've got you."

She moaned, long and loud.

Thank fuck no one else was in the house. It was the most beautiful sound in the world, but I knew what Logan was like. She tucked her head into my shoulder as I continued to press myself against her, extending the pleasure that was coursing through her. Her body slumped into the mattress, her chest heaving. I rolled over, sliding my arm beneath her neck. She rested her head on my chest and slid her leg over mine.

"That was... very..." She was still panting, obviously struggling to find the right word.

"Good?" I asked, looking down at her.

"Very good." She nodded her head, smiling up at me. She looked blissed out. Like she didn't have a care in the world. "Now I know why Bex brags about her orgasms."

I laughed, imagining that. Bragging! She'd make a great match with Logan. They both seemed to have that cheeky, good-natured side to them.

"I didn't imagine this happening after yesterday," she whispered, stroking random patterns on my chest.

"I'm just glad you trusted me enough to listen." I was serious in that statement. Most girls would have kicked me to the curb. Thankfully, Tillie wasn't like them.

"So," she said, nerves creeping into her tone. "Can I ask what does this make us?"

I turned my head, confused.

"I mean, am I your girlfriend or are we just... you know. Fuck buddies or something?"

I didn't register what I was doing until I had rolled her flat on to her back and our lips were back together. I thrust my tongue inside, pressing roughly against hers. The word 'fuck' coming from her mouth turned me into a raging animal.

"You're mine," I whispered. "And I'm yours." I pressed my nose to hers giving it a gentle rub.

"Okay." She grinned up at me with a goofy expression on her face before resting her head back on my chest.

"Yo, lovebirds! Pizza is down here," Chunk yelled up the stairs.

Tillie squeaked in surprise, her worried eyes turning to me.

"Don't worry." I rubbed her arm, soothingly. "They probably grabbed the pizza on their way home."

She nodded and allowed me to pull her from the bed.

Entering the lounge, she went and sat next to Sammy, letting him slide a slice of pizza on a plate for her.

I grinned, watching the exchange. She genuinely seemed to enjoy my brother's company. Logan walked past her, pulling teasingly on her messy bun. She frowned, tightening it back into place.

I walked out into the kitchen where Chunk was opening a few bottles of beer.

"So, how are things?" He grinned, wiggling his eyebrows at me.

"Fine." He was not getting details out of me. Usually we'd laugh and joke and take the piss out of each other but not now. Tillie was different. He rolled his eyes at me, probably thinking I'd turned into an emotional sap, which I had.

"Does she drink beer?" He had a bottle of bud and a mini bottle of juice. She always had juice with her, so it was a good guess.

I grabbed the remaining three bottles. "Why don't you ask her?" I grinned, leaving him to his predicament.

He walked in, holding a bottle of bud and juice out to her. "I didn't know which you'd prefer." He blushed as she smiled up at him.

I don't think I'd ever seen the boss blush before. Ever. Not even around Joy.

"Thank you." She reached for the bottle of bud, taking a swig before biting a mouthful off her pizza.

Chunk smirked, giving me a fist bump. "Good choice, bro."

I grinned, watching her pick the pepperoni off her pizza. Sammy silently held his plate out and she threw them on there. Sammy was a monster for pepperoni. He'd live off the stuff if he could.

"Dude, you're going to have to run twice as fast around that field tomorrow to work that greasy stuff off," Chunk said.

"Yeah, right." Sammy rolled his eyes. "I'm not even on the team yet."

"Think positive," Tillie replied before Chunk or I could say a word. "You'll get there."

Sammy smiled down at her, trusting her.

"That reminds me." Chunk got his wallet out, pulling out two small pieces of card. "This is for you." He handed it to Tillie. "For you to come and watch us at the game next week."

"Thank you." She smiled over at him before her eyes went to me. "Can I bring Bex?"

"Sure." He took a bite off his pizza before continuing. "Joy never comes to our games. They can get a bit loud."

She nodded, tucking the tickets into her jeans. "So, are you boys ready?"

Her question resulted in an hour-long conversation about the plays and the rules of football. The boys were trying to help but it did anything but help. She looked just as confused as she had done at the start of the conversation.

———

DAYS LATER, I still hadn't seen Tillie. We'd gone the whole weekend with only a few texts between us.

At first, I was worried she was starting to push me away after letting me get her off, but she was flat out. She had six essays to get done in the next month plus a life drawing. Watching her run across campus with all her art supplies, I could see the stress was starting to mount.

Getting home from school on Thursday night, I crashed on my bed, feeling the muscles bunch beneath my shirt. Coach was really running us. He knew what we wanted, and he was determined to get us to the championships.

I heard my door creak and couldn't even be bothered to open my eyes.

Please go away.

Before I could move, a small body was leaning over me, its knees pressed on either side of my hips.

"You look exhausted, mister," Tillie whispered in my ear. Her hands settled on my shoulders and began rubbing. Her little fingers dug deep into my knotted-up muscles, trying to release the tension.

I groaned at the sensation, relaxing further into the mattress. Her touch felt like bliss through my shirt. Her hands slid my t-shirt up my ribs, her fingers prodding down my spine. I lifted my arm, grabbing the neck of my tee and pulled it off. She gasped, as her fingers trailed softy over my skin.

I folded my arms in front of me, resting my chin on them. Feeling her fingers trail across my skin caused the most blissful feeling to travel through my veins. Her hand trembled against my back. She was nervous to be touching me. After a few minutes, she pressed her fingers harder, rubbing firm strokes against my muscles.

I groaned, feeling my cock harden, which wasn't comfortable in my current position. Turning over, I settled my hands on her hips, steadying her on top of me. She smiled down at me before her eyes trailed lower. They widened in surprise before meeting mine again.

"Does that... happen a lot?" She tucked her fingers beneath my belt buckle, stabilizing herself on me. "I've never... I don't know... am I doing something wrong? It can't be comfortable for you."

"It's not." I shook my head at her. "You're not doing anything wrong." I sighed, looking up at her. "I just want you too much, is all."

"I'm sorry," she apologized. "I'm trying to..."

"Shhh." I reached up, placing my finger over her lips. "I'm not with you for sex." I shook my head, trying to decide the best way to explain it. "When it happens, I have no doubt it'll be amazing. And I'll want to do it again. And again. And again."

She giggled, her beautiful smile lighting up her face.

"But right now, being with you, without any expectations in the way, is more than enough." I rubbed my hips against her hipbones, letting myself be honest. "I've been with a lot of girls. Some more than others."

She frowned at my words, hurt flashing across her face. I hated seeing it there and worse... being the one to put that look there made me feel like a fool. But she had to know.

"Being with you. Spending time with you. It means more to me than any of those girls. You are more than that."

"I am?" she asked. Sounding so unsure of herself.

"You are." I nodded, staring up at her. "I want to be the same for you. Those girls meant nothing to me. This." I took her hand in mine and slid it up my body until it was over my heart. "This could be everything—to the both of us. I'm willing to try if you are."

She nodded, her eyes shining with unshed tears before bending down and pressing her lips to mine.

I groaned, entwining my hands in the hair flowing down her back, holding her to me. After a few moments, I pulled back, not wanting to be revved up. Just looking at her did that to me. "Want to stay and watch a movie?" I asked, hoping she'd say yes.

She nodded, getting off me. She grabbed her sketchpad out of her bag and joined me back on the bed, lying down so that her head was down by my feet. Opening her pad, she grabbed a pencil and began drawing.

Turning Netflix on, I played the latest episode of Lucifer, knowing how much she enjoyed the program. I placed my hand on her leg, planning to tickle the skin there but that didn't happen. Minutes later, I dozed off, letting my exhaustion win.

It was hours before I woke to a room of darkness. The

only light coming in was from the light under Sammy's door. Looking down, I smiled when I saw Tillie cuddled up against me. We were in the spooning position and it felt perfect.

I nuzzled my nose against her neck, breathing in her sweet, vanilla scent. She stirred, turning her head in my direction.

"How are you still here?" I mumbled, thankful that she was.

"I fell asleep." She chuckled before relaxing again. "I rang Joy near midnight and told her where I was staying. I didn't want her to worry."

"She must really trust me." I chuckled, finding it amusing.

"She does," she whispered. She turned her head and pressed a quick kiss to my cheek. "As do I."

A few moments later, her breathing evened out before sleep took her back under where she remained until morning.

The next morning, I slid my arm gently from beneath her, being extra careful to not wake her. She had slept soundly for the rest of the night. As had I.

After taking a jog around the block, I took a quick shower—a nice, quick and very cold shower before drying off and getting dressed for class. Tillie slept through it all, not even fidgeting when I dropped my bag on the bed.

I grinned, crawling up the bed until I was over her. She looked too fucking cute lying in my bed. Her hair was a mess, sticking up in every direction and had the sexiest little pout on her lips. I couldn't resist. I leaned down, intending on a quick kiss but when I pulled back, she groaned, opening her eyes.

"Good morning." I grinned down at her. She had a 'just fucked' look about her that was making my cock start to come to life.

She looked over at the clock and frowned. "Why are you up so early?" She looked disgusted that it was only seven. She grabbed the blankets and tried pulling them up.

"It's game day. We always get an early morning practice in. Coach says it helps put us in the winning frame of mind." I laughed at her reaction.

"Then why don't 'we' go to practice and I can go back to sleep." She fought with the blankets and this time I let her win. She pulled them up, covering half her face with them.

"Don't I get a good luck kiss?" I teased.

Silence followed for a few minutes before she gave in, pulling the blankets down. She grabbed the collar of my tee and pulled my lips down to hers. I groaned at the feel of her small body beneath mine. She wound her arms around my neck, causing her chest to brush against mine. She was in a thin t-shirt and I could feel her nipples harden.

I pulled my lips back, noticing how red hers were.

"I'll see you later, line-backer." She smiled up at me, tucking the blanket back in around her.

I got up, grabbing my bag and heading for the door. Turning to look at her, I grinned, loving the sight of her there.

"I like waking up with you," I whispered.

Half of me wanted her to hear me and the other half, I admit, was afraid for her to hear me.

Her eyes opened slowly before a small smile graced her face. "Me too."

Leaving her to get an extra hour of sleep, I jogged downstairs, grabbing an apple and waited for the boys. Chunk soon followed and then Sammy.

Logan took the longest looking a lot like Tillie that morning. "This football shit sucks," he groaned, slinging his bag on his back. "Seven in the morning is no time for practice."

I laughed, leading them from the house and leaving a key on the shelf for Tillie.

Logan would never make it as an actual player. I expected he was only in the team for the first year to get extra credits for comparison in his later subjects. He'd make a terrible player with the commitment, but I knew he'd make an excellent sports therapist one day.

11

TILLIE

CLIMBING OUT OF BED, I WANTED NOTHING MORE than to stay there, all day if I could. His bed was so comfy.

Hearing my phone vibrate, I quickly grabbed it out of my bag, cringing at how loud it was.

"Hello?" I hated answering calls off private numbers.

"Hey, chicka!" Bex replied, sounding way too loud and cheery. "Want to have brekkie before class?"

We had a free lesson on Fridays, so our classes didn't usually start until 10:30am.

I nodded before replying. "Sure. Just let me go home and get changed." I cringed at my reply. I didn't want her knowing I had spent the night at Johnny's. She could be like a dog with a bone.

"Go home?" she asked, sounding confused. "Go home. Tillie, where the fuck are you?" She gasped before continuing. "You slept with Johnny!" she screeched, sounding like a wound-up toy.

I cringed, pulling the phone away from my ear. "Calm down. I only fell asleep," I defended. Her comments had me blushing like a stupid little girl that had gotten caught stealing cookies or something.

"Okay." She didn't believe me. "Carter's at nine." She hung up.

Breakfast now sounded like the worst idea ever. I grabbed my bag, pulling my hoodie on and left the house, locking up with the key left on the shelf. Walking in to Joy's, I smiled when I saw her going through a gardening catalogue.

"Hi sweetie," she smiled up at me.

"Thank you for last night." I bent and pressed a kiss to the top of her head. "I fell asleep and was too comfy to move."

She laughed, making me grin. Joy had gotten to know me well enough to know how much I loved a comfy bed. I stood, waiting for her to ask me the awkward questions that I knew Bex was gearing up to ask in just under an hour.

"Everything okay?" she asked, smiling up at me. There was a cheeky sparkle in her eye, but she never asked or hinted at anything. "Are you going to the game tonight?"

"Yes, Chunk got me a ticket."

She frowned at my response.

"Is that okay?"

"Of course. I forgot to tell you that I'm away this weekend. A few of us ladies had booked tickets to go and see a play." She looked worried at the thought of leaving me on my own.

"Oh, that's cool," I enthused, trying to make her feel better. "Have a good time!"

She relaxed at my words, going back to browsing through her catalogue.

Jogging upstairs, I took a quick shower and changed, throwing my hair up in a bun.

After wishing Joy safe travels, I left the house, making sure to grab the keys. Making my way to Carter's Café, I resolved to be honest with Bex. Sex was obviously a touchy subject for me and it wasn't like I could talk to Joy about it. I wondered if Bex might be able to offer some good advice.

Walking in, I grinned at Bex, who sat in a booth at the back, waving enthusiastically at me. There couldn't have been more than ten people inside. I grinned, sitting across from her, smiling at the waitress coming to our table with a latte for Bex and a steaming hot chocolate with extra chocolate sprinkles for me.

"I ordered the pancakes with extra bacon for you." She grinned at me, knowing me all too well.

"Thanks, Bex." I smiled at her, laughing when I saw a blush steal over her cheeks. She blushed over the craziest things. "So," she said, shaking her head. "Give me the details."

I cocked an eyebrow at her, trying to act clueless. "I only slept."

She rolled her eyes at me. "Seriously? You had that piece of fine ass in a bed, all to yourself, and you're trying to tell me you only slept? What the fuck? You should have been climbing him like a pole."

I laughed, loving her enthusiasm. The more I hung

out with Bex, the more I was convinced that she would be perfect for Logan. Shame she was into girls.

"So," she said quietly. "What's the problem?" She smiled at me, trying to make me comfortable I think.

"I don't know." I shrugged my shoulders, not knowing how to explain it. "I just... I don't think I'm ready for it."

She looked confused.

"He's been with so many and what if I'm not enough?" It was a simple question and one I felt comfortable enough with Bex to ask. What if I wasn't enough? What if, by morning, I was another notch on his belt? It would kill me. I'd become the laughing stock of the entire college. What if, deep down, he realized he would prefer someone like Lucy?

"Tillie." She reached over, taking my hand in hers. "That boy is in love with you."

Was she high? I shook my head, disagreeing with her. It was just a crush, that's all.

"I'm serious," she continued. "I've seen the way he watches you. Not only has he stopped sleeping around, he doesn't even look at another girl. I bent over in front of him to pick up a pencil—just to test him—and he just freaking looked around me to watch the door. He's like a little puppy waiting for the next treat."

I laughed at her choice of words. Was she serious? Could he be as crazy about me as I was about him? I couldn't lie. I had created a wall to protect myself, but I wanted to trust him.

"You have a good heart, Till. Don't lock it away. Open it up and let him in."

I looked at her, trying to believe her words.

"If he screws up, I promise to personally whip his ass." She gave me a cheeky wink, making me giggle.

Breakfast quickly arrived, and it was delicious. I could have lived off pancakes and bacon, especially if the bacon was crispy. It was the food of the gods.

"That reminds me. I have a ticket for you." I took it out of my purse, sliding it across the table to her. "Please say you'll come with me. I don't want to go alone."

"I suppose I can be seen with you." She rolled her eyes before grinning at me. "We can meet there around six?"

I nodded, agreeing with the plan.

Hours later, I was rushing from classes, my mind turning over my last subject. I cringed at how the professor favored life drawings over landscapes. Apparently, landscapes were not suited to today's environment. We now lived in the digital age and sitting in front of landscapes capturing the detail was to be considered a thing of the past, especially since we had such advanced software like Photoshop.

What a twit! How did he not realize that using digital software to create landscape drawings was sick. That should be a thing of the past. I would choose sitting in front of lush green fields capturing the beauty of a windmill turning in the wind any day of the week. It relaxed me—made me feel at ease. It was one of the many things I used to do with my mother. No matter how many times I would drag her somewhere to draw, she would never complain. She would always just sit patiently and wait until I was done. She was where my love of drawing came from and I was never going to give that part of my skill up.

Walking inside, I dropped my bag on the armchair and ran upstairs to my room. I had just enough time for a quick shower and change before meeting Bex. Stripping in the bathroom, I jumped in the shower doing a quick soap up and jumping back out. Wrapping a towel around my body, I froze when I got to my doorway.

On my bed, was a blue box with a white bow on top. Tucked beneath the ribbon was a note written in Johnny's handwriting.

Please wear me

I grinned, pulling the lid off and gasped at what was inside. It was an exact replica of Johnny's jersey except the front had his jersey number, number ten, and '#1' on the back. I loved it! I knew Lucy and her minions would hate it and it would probably send me to the top of their most hated list, but it would be worth it. Johnny obviously put enough thought into it for me to wear it.

After a quick change, I grabbed my cream cardigan and left the house, locking up and making my way toward the sports arena. Standing outside, I looked around, trying to spot Bex. The place was packed with crowds of people. I was surprised that so many were there but then remembered this was a town that loved their football players.

I spotted Lucy up ahead, cringing at the smirk she sent my way. I really didn't want any contact with her that night. Confrontation and I did not get along. My gawking was quickly interrupted when Bex appeared in my view. I laughed at how her face was painted with the school colors on her cheeks.

"Problem?" She cocked an eyebrow at me. "We turned lesbian all of a sudden?"

"What?" I looked at her confused.

"You and Lucy having a stare down. Wasn't sure if you wanted to rip each other's clothes off or pounce on each other."

I rolled my eyes at her lame joke. "Ha ha. Very funny."

She laughed, looping her arm with mine and pulling me toward the entrance. Taking our seats, I laughed at her. She was looking so cocky with the team's logos painted on her cheeks.

"I look fabulous, right?" She grinned at me, showing off her pearly whites.

The stands started filling up. A few people stared at us, but most of them were chatting amongst themselves. Some had their faces painted, but mostly everyone just looked excited.

"So, do you know the rules of football?" I hoped she did because I had no clue.

She shook her head before her eyes moved past me. She widened her eyes, nodding her head forward for me to look.

I turned my head and froze when I saw Johnny climbing the steps. He was dressed in his football jersey and tight trousers. He even had his shoulder pads on and was carrying his helmet.

Fuck, he was sexy.

He high-fived a few members of the crowd before his eyes landed on me. He gave me a sexy wink before continuing in our direction. What the hell was he doing? He should be in the changing rooms or something.

He stopped next to me, going down on one knee and placing his helmet on my lap.

"Is everything okay?" I asked, quietly.

I noticed people beginning to gawk at Johnny in the crowds. I guess he did not do this all the time. Even people a few blocks down were turning to look. Some were even standing. They were acting like he was an NFL player already or something.

"You ready for your first game?" He grinned at me, looking every inch the professional football player.

I'd never seen the attraction with footballers before but looking at Johnny, I had been converted.

"I think so." I grinned at him, trying to ignore the stares from around us, including from Bex.

"Take your cardigan off," he said, reaching for my hand.

"What?" I chuckled, feeling very confused.

"It's not too cold," he reasoned. "Plus, nobody is going to see how fucking amazing you look in *your* jersey." He emphasized the word 'your'. "It's yours and no one else's." His eyes bored into mine, making me swoon.

I reached up, slipping my cardigan off. The second my back became exposed, the whispers started up. I guess the '#1' said a lot.

"That's better." He grinned up at me, entwining his fingers with mine. "Kiss me."

I laughed at him, thinking he was joking. When he

only continued to look at me with that carefree smile on his face, I cringed.

Seriously? He expected me to kiss him in front of the entire freaking arena?!

"Ooh, look, look!" Bex said, taking my attention from Johnny. She was pointing at the big massive screen at the top of the field.

Kill me now.

I was on the screen with Johnny. A live fucking camera feed.

I looked back to him, expecting to see a cocky smirk on his face, but I didn't. He was looking at me like I was his whole world. It was the same look every Disney prince wore when looking at their princess. I sighed, wanting to believe Bex's words from earlier but it was hard when you go from being a loner to the centre of someone's world as Bex would put it.

"Kiss your fella!" Bex demanded, bumping me with her elbow. She widened her eyes at me, trying to convince me to take the bait.

Looking back to Johnny, I was resolved to do just that. It wasn't like I hated kissing Johnny. Honestly, I could die a happy death doing that all day. Before I could make a move, he took my chin in between his forefinger and thumb. He pulled my face closer to his, fusing our lips together. He kept it sweet and short, thankfully, before pulling away from me. One last wink and he was jogging back down the stairs to a roaring applause.

The live camera screen followed him, leaving me and my embarrassment behind.

Bex was staring at me with her mouth wide open. "So

fucking hot," she whispered, dramatically fanning herself.

"Shut up," I chuckled, focusing back on the field.

I cringed when my eyes settled on Lucy. Even from this far away, the girl did not look happy. Downright pissed would have been a good way to describe her.

The music started up, blasting through the speakers and the players slowly filtered on to the field. Individual announcements were done for all the main players, where the back-up players just ran to the bench and sat down. The crowd went wild for most of them, but it was deafening when Johnny was introduced. It was clear who the main attraction was there.

An hour later, we were nearly at the end of the game. To me it was already over. The score was 73-30, but my boys were well in the lead.

"So," Bex started. "Are you going to be at the party later?"

"Party?" I hadn't heard anything about a party.

"Seriously?" She rolled her eyes at my naivety. "Every game comes with a party."

I shrugged my shoulders dismissively. "I hadn't really thought about it." I couldn't remember Johnny saying anything about a party.

Thirty minutes later, he had scored twelve more points with a touchdown, ending the game on 85-39. The crowd were straight on their feet, cheering and clapping for their winning team. I smiled when I saw Johnny and the boys line up and shake the other team's hands. They may have been competitive, but they seemed to be good boys as well.

Bex and I remained in our seats, deciding to wait for Johnny. I had no clue what the plan was for after so waiting for him seemed like the best plan. Half an hour later we were still sitting there, wrapped in our cardigans.

"What the hell is taking so long?" Bex complained, her hands shaking from the cold. "They having pedicures or some shit?"

I laughed, leaving my seat and beginning the walk down. Maybe it'd be warmer down by the changing rooms. Walking on to the field, I cringed when I heard female voices coming from the side of the changing room block. I turned around, trying to avoid bumping into the snotty cheerleaders when Bex forced my arm through hers, stopping me from escaping.

Lucy walked around the side of the block with a few of her cheerleaders on either side of her. They were all still dressed in their slutty outfits. Lucy opened her mouth to say something—probably an insult—when Logan and Sammy jogged out of the building, mock-punching each other in the arm. I grinned at their antics before Logan saw me.

"There she is." He grinned over at me before jogging toward us.

I held my arms out for him, expecting him to want a hug when he went straight past me, instead hugging Bex and swinging her around in a circle. I laughed at them. They were perfect for each other. They just didn't know it. Instead I took the hug off Sammy. He was acting like a champ. He may not have gotten to play that night, but he wasn't letting it get him down.

"The team played well tonight." I smiled at him, letting him rest his arm across my shoulders.

"They did." He grinned down at me. "He'll be out in a few."

I opened my mouth to reply when a high-pitched nasal voice sounded from behind us.

"Aren't you with the wrong brother, Tillie?" She smirked at me. "Or do they share you around?" Lucy's friend giggled at the jab.

Sammy immediately dropped his arm, positioning himself in front of me. I put my arm on his, not wanting him to say anything to make it worse. Before he could, Johnny walked out of the door, walking straight past Lucy and her snobby friends. Sammy relaxed immediately, causing me to relax.

"Don't worry, ladies." He grinned, walking straight to me. "She knows which brother she belongs to." He didn't hesitate in placing his hands at the back of my thighs and hoisting me up.

I was not a massive fan of public displays of affection, but I was finding it easier with Johnny every time he kissed me. I leaned my head down, wrapping my arms around his shoulders and pressing my lips to his. He hummed against my lips, pressing his tongue against mine before ending the kiss.

"Congrats, Mr. Line-Backer." I grinned down at him, feeling very proud of him. He'd played like a pro.

"Thank you." He smiled up at me, his hands firmly holding my thighs. "Do I get a reward?" His eyes smouldered with lust.

I say lust because I could feel something firm press

against me. I brazenly rubbed myself against him, gasping at the feel of him.

Opening my eyes, I looked down at him. "I'm sure we can think of something," I whispered, brushing the hair away from his face. It was a flirtatious response which was very unlike me, but it was the truth. Since breakfast with Bex this morning, I had thought of nothing else but trying to open myself up to Johnny.

"Let's get this show on the road!" Logan cheered from behind Johnny.

Johnny slowly put me down, taking my hand in his and began leading the way home.

"So, where are we going now?" I asked.

"I thought we could go to the party and hang out with the team a little." He cocked an eyebrow at me, waiting for my response.

I nodded, tightening my grasp on Johnny's hand.

He and I told Bex, Sammy and Logan that we'd see them at the party.

As we walked inside Johnny's house, he pulled me toward the stairs. "Let me get changed quickly and we can go," he said, placing his foot on the first step.

"I'll wait here." I pulled my hand from his, refusing to be pulled up those stairs. I went weak at the knees whenever I saw that man topless.

He grinned, jogging up the stairs and disappearing into his room. Half a minute later, he was back out, pulling a black tee down over his abs.

I spun around, rolling my eyes at myself. He obviously knew my secret.

He took my hand and we left the house, making our

way down the street. At the end was a fraternity house that some of the team lived at. Walking in, Johnny was greeted by several party-goers with pats on the back and hand-shakes. He tightened his grip on mine, pulling me closer.

Looking around, I didn't recognize a single person. They were obviously mostly college students but there were no art students in sight. Walking into the kitchen, I grinned at Sammy. He was filling drinks for him and Logan who currently had his tongue half way down some random girl's throat. Bex sat on the worktop, knocking back drink after drink. I noticed she had her hand tucked into Sammy's jean pocket on his ass.

I cocked my eyebrow at Johnny, making him laugh. "I thought she was a lesbian," I whispered quietly.

He took a gulp of his beer bottle that Sammy had passed him. "News to me." He shook his head, clearing his thoughts. "Maybe she's experimenting."

Sammy turned to pass me the drink. Taking a sniff, I smiled when a strawberry scent hit me. I hummed at the taste. There was a slight taste of vodka, but it was mostly fruity. I followed Johnny into the lounge where he led me to the snooker table located to the right. He put his bottle on the oak ledge and turned, placing his hands on my hips and lifted me until I was sitting on the table.

I grinned up at him, appreciating the gesture. I was too short to have been able to jump up there myself. He placed his hand on my thigh, taking another gulp of his drink, and I placed my hand on his, trying to stop the tingles from traveling up my leg. With one touch, he had turned me into a quivering mess.

Johnny's attention was quickly pulled from mine when Bex waved him over to her. He frowned, passing me his bottle and walking over to her. She gave me a small smile before turning her back to talk to Johnny.

It was rude to stare but I couldn't turn away. Bex's head was nodding up and down before Johnny's eyes shot over her head to look at me. I was expecting a smile, but he looked back at Bex too quickly. He nodded, gave her a small smile and walked back over to me.

What was that about?

I held his bottle out to him, smiling when he took it. "Is everything okay?" I asked.

"Of course." He put his hand back on my leg, holding it out for mine. Entwining our fingers together, the tingle quickly returned.

A few minutes later, he drained the rest of his bottle, tossing it in the bin just in front of us. "Do you want to leave?" he asked, turning to me. He looked so open and honest.

My eyes went to the door where Bex still stood. I smiled when she held her hands up giving me the thumbs up symbol. I took a deep breath, feeling the nerves settle in my stomach. "Okay." I nodded at him, letting him help me down.

Leaving the house together, I felt nervous to be alone with Johnny.

Just the two of us.

Alone.

12

JOHNNY

Hanging at the party was not something I wanted to be doing, especially with Joy being away for the weekend. Having Tillie to myself for a few hours was something I had thought about all day long. The only reason I was there at all was because of Tillie. I didn't want her to seize up or pull away from me.

Lifting her up on the table made me feel like a man—like her man. Standing at her side, my eyes traveled around the room. I could see a few of the boys checking her out. Feeling her little hand press over mine, I grinned, feeling cocky.

That's right, fuckers! Look elsewhere.

I didn't like or want to be territorial with Tillie. Hell knew she'd had more than a few people to worry about with me when I had slept with more than half of the campus already.

I frowned, looking toward the kitchen. Tillie's friend was waving enthusiastically at me. At first, I thought it was Tillie she wanted, but her eyes remained on mine. I passed my bottle to Tillie before walking over to her. I turned my back to the kitchen, not really wanting anyone to hear whatever this was about. I hadn't seen Bex since the other day when I'd been doing the mad dash looking for Tillie. Thinking back, I hadn't exactly got the warmest reaction from her.

"Everything okay?" I asked, crossing my arms over my chest.

"Yeah, fine." She waved her hand, dismissively. "Why are you guys here?"

"Excuse me?" What the hell was her problem?

"Joy is away for the weekend and you're hanging out at a party?" She was not impressed. "I took Tillie to breakfast this morning."

My eyes shot over her head, looking at Tillie. She smiled at me, looking sexy as hell wearing that jersey. I looked back to Bex quickly, not wanting to sport an erection in front of Tillie's only girlfriend.

"She's afraid you're going to drop her as soon as you've had her." She cocked her eyebrow at me. "If you do, I will take great pleasure in removing your testicles."

Fuck! I placed my hands in front of me, trying to protect it from her words.

"Be good to her, Johnny. She's been through a lot." She jerked her head backwards to Tillie, dismissing me.

I chuckled internally at her forceful but scary tone. I was glad Tillie had her. She loved her just like a best friend should.

I took my bottle from Tillie, placing my hand back in

its spot on her lap. She placed her hand over mine again. I felt small tingles shoot up my arm at her touch.

"Is everything okay?" she asked, worry in her tone.

"Of course." I nodded my head, stealing my resolve to not tell her about that conversation with Bex. I'd never live it down.

I brought the bottle to my mouth, gulping it down. Trying to focus on anything else but crawling on top of her on this snooker table. The frat boys wouldn't be impressed, although, knowing these boys, they'd probably enjoy it.

Tossing my bottle in the bin, I took a deep breath before turning to her.

"Do you want to leave?" I asked.

This was all on Tillie's time. All of my balls were in her court as far as I was concerned.

"Okay." She nodded at me, giving me a small smile.

I grinned, helping her down off the table and taking her hand in mine. Walking down the street, I smiled down at her. I know Bex had had sex on her mind when she was talking to me, and as much as it was on my mind, it wasn't why I wanted to be alone with her. I had resolved to wait as long as I needed to. It wasn't only about getting my dick wet as it always had been in the past.

It was just about being with her.

No matter what we were doing.

We got to my house and I opened the gate, intending to lead her up the path but she resisted. She stood still, pulling on my arm. Had she changed her mind?

"Is everything okay?" I was trying to keep soft and

gentle as a part of our time together when all I wanted to do was ravage her as she should be. She was completely unaware of the effect she had on the opposite sex.

She looked up at me, dipping her tongue out to wet her bottom lip. "Can we..." Her eyes flicked across the street before coming back to mine. "Joy isn't home?"

She phrased it like a question, but I knew what she was saying. At Joy's, it would just be the two of us. No interruptions. No roommates sneaking around. Just me and her.

I nodded, letting her lead me across the street to her house. I stood back, waiting for her to unlock the door. I didn't want to crowd her, but I also didn't want to be this far away from her either. I followed her inside and walked into the lounge on the left, and slipping my jacket off, I placed it over the back of the armchair.

Tillie stood at the bottom of the stairs, holding her hand out to me.

I took it, not hesitating. I'd follow her to hell and back if I had to.

She led me up, entering her bedroom.

I smiled, looking around. There were sketch pads all over the place, pencils, empty pots of glitter and crumpled up pieces of paper by the bin. I walked over to the desk, picking up a piece of paper. It was covered in lines and curves. I smiled when I recognized the magic number ten. The crowds at football games often shouted that at me when it came time to kick the ball up the field. I found that it spurred me on, made me work harder. I was amazed at how detailed this sketch was. She had even begun to add color to it: light grey to the jersey and yellow on the number.

"It's not finished yet," she whispered, standing a few steps behind me in the middle of the room.

I put it back down and turned. She was fidgeting where she was. The sleeves of her cardigan were pulled down to the very ends of her arms so that only the tops of her fingers were showing. She was nibbling her lip, her teeth digging in to the plumpness that I wanted to nibble on.

Walking over to her, I took her hands in mine.

She tipped her head up, looking into mine.

"Kiss me," she whispered.

I leaned down, pressing my lips to hers softly. She sucked my bottom lip in between hers. She parted her lips, allowing my tongue entry to press against hers. I unclasped my hands from hers, trailing my fingers up her arms until I was holding her face in my palms.

She reached up, pulling the collars of her cardigan until I trailed my hands down, taking over. I slid it down her arms and slung it over the back of her office chair. Looking down, she had me ready to come undone. She looked so fucking sexy in that jersey it made me want to rip it off her.

I tensed my hands into fists, trying to stay calm. "You're so fucking beautiful," I whispered.

She cringed before looking down at our feet and I pulled her face back to mine.

"Don't hide from me." I pressed my lips back to hers and began walking her backwards toward the bed. Her fingers tightened on my tee, holding herself to me.

We stopped by the bed. I didn't want to move too fast, but Tillie had me so wound up. She had my engine revving and I didn't want it to stop. She kicked her shoes off, before sitting down on the bed. She scooted back until her head was lying on the pillow.

I crawled over her, moving my lips back to hers. Her hands latched onto the button of my jeans before snapping them open. I looked down at her, surprised that she was taking the first step.

"Are you sure?" I asked.

She nodded, dipping her hand inside and stroking her fingers against me.

Fuck.

This girl had me ready to blow with one touch. I grabbed the hem of her jersey, meeting her eyes before pulling it up, and she nodded, arching her back for me to move it and raising her arms.

Tossing it to the floor, I groaned at the sight before me: she was wearing a sexy blue bra with silver trim, her tits pushed into the sexiest v-shaped cleavage. I traced my finger over the crease of her cleavage, loving the shiver that ran through her.

I pulled back, standing up and pulling my tee off.

Her eyes immediately dropped to my chest before dipping lower to my abs. I wasn't conceited or vain, but I worked hard for this body. The fact that she was looking at it with that expression on her face had me shaking with pure lust.

I placed my fingers on my zip, looking at Tillie. Discarding my shoes and jeans, I froze when her little fingers went to the button on her jeans. She pulled the zip down, and my hands immediately gripped the bottom of her jeans and pulled them down.

She made a surprised noise at the contact, her body moving down the bed a little due to my firm grip. She reached her arms up, grabbing onto the slats of her headboard. I grinned at how little she was on that bed.

She nodded, her chest heaving slowly. "Turn out the light," she whispered, her eyes flicking to the doorway.

I quickly shut the door, turning the light off before rejoining her on the bed. Lying down next to her, we both stared at the ceiling. It was completely dark, the only light coming in from the moon outside.

"We can stop at any time," I whispered, turning to look at her.

"No." She shook her head, turning to face me. "I want to. I trust you but I just..." She took a deep breath, looking back to the ceiling. "Just don't break me."

I slid my arm beneath her, pulling her body over to me until she was positioned above me. I settled my hands on her hips, groaning when she rotated her hips against me. I could feel how wet she was through her panties. Her hands rested on my chest, her fingers rubbing back and forth in small strokes.

"I won't." I looked up at her, trying to find the words. "Since meeting you, you have captured me—mind, heart, body and soul. You are all I think about."

"Really?" she asked.

Was she serious? How could she not know? Did she not know what she meant to me? How important she had become? She plagued my thoughts day and night. I didn't think I loved her—it hadn't been long enough—but staring down at her, I realized it would be so easy to love her.

I leaned down, pressing my lips to hers, softly sucking on her bottom lip. "I won't hurt you," I whispered against her lips, my hands latching onto her hips.

Her mouth slowly trailed down to my neck, kissing, biting and licking.

I groaned, my hips bucking off the bed. I trailed my hands up over her ribs until I met the clasp of her bra. I unclipped it, wanting to see her. Needing to feel her skin against mine.

She sat back, holding her hands crossed over her chest. She looked so vulnerable. I could see a bit of worry in her eyes, but she had nothing to worry about. She kept comparing herself to Lucy's standards, but she had to realize that Lucy had fuck all compared to my Tillie. She didn't even compare.

She slowly lowered her arms, letting me pull the offending item off her. Tossing it to the floor, my hands followed, massaging her breasts. They were fucking perfect. I expected them to be smaller due to how tiny she was, but they were the perfect handful.

She gasped, tipping her head back and rocking against my stomach.

Fuck.

She was very responsive.

I twisted her nipples, pinching and pulling. They were already erect before I touched them. My cock was rock hard, standing at attention against her ass. It was uncomfortable being trapped in my boxers, but I ignored it, wanting to make her first time special.

I slid my one hand down her stomach, needing to feel her. I knew she was soaking wet but all I could think about was feeling her with my fingers. I pressed my thumb against her clit over her panties, rubbing in a circular motion.

She moaned, long and hard at my touch, her nails digging into my chest.

"Do you like that?" I asked, whispering.

She nodded, grinding herself harder against me.

I rolled us over, lying in between her legs. I dipped my head, my mouth eager to taste her skin. I sucked her nipple into my mouth, kissing and licking her tender flesh.

She moaned, her neck arching. She bent her legs up further, allowing me to fit more comfortably between them. I rested my chin on her chest bone, needing to see her reaction. I trailed my hand down over her belly, dipping my finger in her belly button making her giggle. My girl was ticklish.

As I slid my finger beneath her panties, she sucked in a breath. I continued, sliding my fingers down further. There was a tiny patch of curls before my fingers met her warmth. I groaned at the feel of her. She was soaking wet. Sliding my finger down further, I smirked when I heard the noise of my fingers moving in between her folds. Rubbing her back and forth was getting my dick excited.

Down boy.

She moaned, her legs parting further.

"Okay?" I asked. It was a stupid question to ask because she obviously was, but I had to move slowly with

Tillie. She may not have known it, but she was it for me. I couldn't imagine doing this with anyone else.

She nodded, running her hand through my hair. Her hips rotated, wanting more.

I slid my middle finger inside, groaning at the heat that instantly wrapped around my finger. I pulled it in and out a few times before adding a second digit. Dropping my forehead to her chest, I realized I was in both heaven and hell: hell, because all I could imagine was feeling that around my cock; heaven because she felt fucking amazing.

As I pumped my fingers in and out, she began rotating her pelvis.

Fuck, she was beautiful.

"Do you like that?" I asked. I didn't even give her chance to reply. The filter between my mouth and brain had disappeared having her beneath me. "Feel how tight you are. You're so fucking wet."

She moaned, tossing her head back into the pillow, holding my head to her chest.

I sucked the flesh of her breast, my teeth sinking in. It wasn't my plan to mark her or anything, but the little minx had me so turned on, I was ready to explode. I slid my fingers in further, feeling her start to tighten even more.

I turned my wrist, pumping my fingers in further. I curled them upwards, trying to find that spot to make her see stars. She gasped before letting out a long moan, her muscles clamping down on my fingers. I gently moved them inside her, trying to prolong her pleasure.

Pulling them out, I lay down next to her, unable to stop staring at her.

Her cheeks were flushed with pleasure and she was panting. Her hair was all over the place. 'Just fucked' described her perfectly in that moment. She turned on her side to face me.

My eyes shot down to her chest. The action of her turning over didn't help my cock. It mashed her tits together making my cock protest. He wanted inside her.

I leaned over, pressing my lips to her quickly before excusing myself to the bathroom.

Shutting the door, I groaned, pulling my boxers down a little for my cock to escape. It finally felt like I could breathe again. It looked angry with its purple head. I grasped my cock, pumping slowly. Closing my eyes, I had the same image on repeat going round and round in my head. Tillie beneath me. Tillie riding me. Tillie against the shower wall. Tillie on her knees sucking my cock.

Tillie. Tillie. Tillie.

I was pumping my cock fast and hard, imagining her on top of me, riding me.

Fuck, it wasn't going to last. I grabbed a wad of toilet paper, and holding it over the head of my cock, I moved my head back, leaning against the wall. I groaned, coming against the paper when one last image flashed through my mind. Tillie in my jersey. In only my jersey.

Fuck.

Looking up, I saw my reflection staring back at me. My cheeks were red, and my chest was heaving. I looked like I had been running a marathon.

I tossed the paper in the toilet before taking a quick

piss. Washing my hands, I wiped my hands in the towel before wiping my chest. The sweat was pouring out of me.

Walking back to Tillie, I shut the door, smiling at the sight in front of me. She was still in the same position but this time she was tucked beneath the blankets. Getting back into bed, she turned to me, laying her head on my chest.

"You okay?" I asked before wrapping my arm around her.

She slid her leg over mine, making me tense. Fuck. She'd been wearing panties when I left her. I felt her warmth against my skin.

"Yeah." She looked up at me, the moon from outside shining down through the gap in the curtains. "Thank you."

"For what?" I was confused and trying hard to ignore her heat that was doing its best to wake my cock up.

"For being you." She smiled up at me, making me smile back. "I didn't know it could feel like that."

"You don't regret it then?" I cocked an eyebrow at her, teasing her.

She shook her head enthusiastically, making me laugh. Cuddling her head back into my chest, I relaxed my shoulders, trying to think of unattractive things to keep my cock down.

"Are you going to make love to me?" she asked, her voice a whisper.

I was shocked she'd asked. I never thought she would. I couldn't deny that I was thinking of nothing else, but I hadn't wanted to push her. If she'd been happy with what happened tonight, then that's where I would have left it, but no way did I want my girl unsatisfied.

"Is that what you want?" I asked, looking down at her.

She nodded her head, peeking her Bambi eyes up at me.

I must have stared at her for a beat too long before taking her hand in mine and pulling her closer. I didn't stop until she was positioned over me, throwing the blanket back.

"Are you sure?" I asked, rubbing my thumbs along her hip bones.

"I am." She leaned down, pressing her lips to mine.

I grabbed her hips, pulling her up my body a little so that I could get rid of my boxers. Kicking them off, I kept a tight grip on her, not wanting to knock her off the bed.

She giggled at the movement but cut off to a moan when my mouth sucked her nipple into my mouth. I couldn't get enough of her tits. I had always been an ass man in the past, but her tits were now the focus of my attention. Grabbing her other breast, I twisted her nipple, pulling and pinching. Switching breasts, I groaned at her taste. She even tasted like vanilla.

She moaned, threading her fingers into the back of my hair, holding my head into her chest. She loved me worshipping her delectable tits.

I took hold of her hips, pulling her down the bed a little. I groaned, feeling her hand against my cock.

"I think you on top would be better the first time." I looked up at her, noticing how uncertain she looked.

"But I..." She sighed, rubbing her forehead. "I've never done this before."

"I know, baby. But this way, you'll be in control." I rubbed my hand up and down her thigh in a soothing gesture. "We can stop at any time."

She nodded, placing her hands on my shoulders.

"Are you..." I looked down at her tits briefly. "Do you want me to...?"

"I'm on the pill," she whispered. "I mean, I'm okay... if you are..."

I frowned, confused. Did she know we would be doing this?

"My dad..." She rolled her eyes at herself. "It was part of our deal. The only way he'd agree for me to go to college so far away from him. He didn't want me going home knocked up." She chuckled, trying to make light of it.

Fuck, was she serious? Was she truly offering herself to me? Just me and her with no barriers?

"I'm clean," I whispered. "If you want to."

She nodded her head before lowering herself down.

I tried to refrain from pushing up against her. This had to be her show.

I grasped my dick, holding it steady and positioning it at her entrance. She pushed down slowly, letting my cock slide in.

Fuck. She felt amazing. Her tightness wrapped around me, making my eyes roll back. I groaned, loving the feel of her. I looked up, checking that she was okay.

She slid down further, letting her heat envelop me. We both froze when I'd gone as far as I could before meeting her barrier. This part was going to hurt. She gave me a small nod, urging me to help.

I tilted my pelvis, gently sliding my cock further inside her. She tensed, her teeth digging into her lip. I reached up, grasping her breasts and massaging them. If this could take her mind off some of the pain, I'd gladly do it.

After a few minutes, she supported her hips, urging herself further down. She moaned, her back arching, her chest pushing out. She rocked up and down slowly, becoming accustomed to the feeling.

A few thrusts later, she was moving with firmer strokes, grinding herself against me. I groaned, loving the sight of her above me. I lifted my hips up, needing to go deeper. We got so lost in staring at each other that we must have moved at the same time, sending my cock even deeper inside of her.

I groaned, my back arching at the feeling of her wrapped around me. I sat up, my lips seeking out the soft flesh of her breasts. Taking hold of her hips, I helped lift her up and down on me, sending firmer strokes deep inside of her. She moaned, long and loud, threading her fingers into the back of my hair before bending my head back and slamming her lips down on mine.

The only sounds in the room were our lips meeting, breaths panting and the sound of us moving together. I could feel my balls beginning to tighten but I had to hold out.

I lifted my hips, doing shorter and firmer strokes. I could feel her inner muscles begin to quiver. I massaged her breasts, pulling on her nipples before sliding my hand down and paying special attention to her clit. As I gave it a gentle flick, she half-moaned, half-shrieked as she came around me, making me come inside her.

I collapsed back on the bed with Tillie lying on my chest. We were both panting as though we had run a marathon.

"That was..." She let out a heavy breath, not bothering to finish her sentence.

"Good, right?" I chuckled, smoothing the hair away from her forehead before pressing a tender kiss there.

"Fucking fantastic!" she enthused.

I laughed, wrapping my arms around her.

Looks like my girl had a potty mouth when she was high on orgasms.

13

TILLIE

Rolling over in bed, I groaned, my tense muscles aching. A shower was needed. Opening my eyes, I expected to be greeted with a very fit sight of Johnny next to me. Instead, I was met with a very cold side of the bed. My bedroom door was wide open, and his clothes were gone. I tried swallowing past the lump in my throat at the disappointment I felt.

I guess he got what he'd wanted.

Like a stupid slut, I gave it freely.

I pulled my jersey on, sniffing the collar like a pathetic girl. I loved that his scent clung to it. Walking out of the room, I cringed at the soreness between my legs. Damn, no wonder half the campus had slept with him. He really knew what to do in the bedroom department.

Walking downstairs, I reasoned to just get on with it. So, I made a stupid mistake. Ignoring him shouldn't be that hard—even if he did live across the street—as he'd probably move on to the next girl on his list.

Walking into the kitchen, I shrieked at the sight in front of me. The worktop was filled with a selection of pancakes, blueberries, bacon, juice and coffee. There were also three fit guys hanging around in there.

"Well, hello, sleepy head," Logan said, waggling his eyebrows up and down. His eyes trailed down to my legs before going back up. "Have fun?"

I stared at him with shock, my mouth gaping open. What the hell? Was it that obvious?

Sammy walked closer to him and punched him in the arm. Hard.

"Leave her alone, dude." He turned to me, smiling. "Hi, Tillie."

He offered a small glass of orange juice to me. I took it, mouthing a small thank you to him.

"There she is." Johnny turned from the cooker, grinning at me before walking toward me. "Morning." He bent down, giving me a sweet kiss.

"Morning." I gave him a small smile before looking back at our guests. I cleared my throat, trying to pull my jersey down a little. It was awkward because Sammy was staring at my legs and Logan was just smirking at me.

"Alright, boys." Johnny turned around, positioning his body in front of me. "Time's up. You can go home now." He pointed at the back door.

I giggled behind him. He sounded like their father instead of their room-mate. The next thing I heard was the boys moving before a chorus of goodbyes sounded.

"So." Johnny took my hand and led me over to the

worktop. "I didn't know what you'd like so I made everything." He looked so nervous. It was kind of cute seeing the popular line-backer nervous in front of me. He lifted me up, setting me on a chair. He grabbed my legs, gently lifting them up before stepping in between them. "You look so fucking sexy in that top." His lips trailed down to my neck, kissing and licking my skin. I moaned, loving the feel of his lips on my neck. He seemed to know exactly which parts of me to pay attention to.

Just then, the coffee machine beeped, causing him to sigh into my neck. My hands tensed on his sides, the action going straight to where I wanted him—where he obviously wanted to be as well considering how tight his jeans looked.

He pulled away from me, pouring himself a coffee. He dished some pancakes up for the both of us before adding some crispy rashers of bacon to mine.

I dug in, moaning at the taste. "This is delicious!" I enthused.

"So…" He cleared his throat before wiping his lips with a napkin. He reached over and took my hand in his. "Did you think I had left this morning?"

I must have taken too long to answer when he continued.

"You looked a little shocked to see me in your kitchen." He cocked an eyebrow at me, waiting.

I sighed. Honesty was the best policy, right? I nodded slowly, looking into his green eyes.

"I thought so." He turned his body, looking at me sideways. "I'm not going anywhere. Okay?" Another cocked eyebrow. "Last night was…" He shook his head, as if to clear his thoughts. "I know how important last night was. Being with you—being your first—I know how important that was. I'm with you for as long as you'll have me."

My eyes filled with unshed tears at his words. Johnny looked like a hard-core football player, but he was a real sweetheart. I was counting myself lucky to have found him. Leaning forward, I pressed my lips to his.

HOURS LATER, I was cleaning the lounge area and polishing all the surfaces. Johnny had gone home to get some studying done and in his place, Bex was lounging on the sofa.

"So," I said, sitting in Joy's armchair. "What happened with Sammy last night?"

She looked over at me confused. "Sammy?"

"Yeah." I rolled my eyes at how disinterested she looked. "You know, the guy whose ass pockets you had your hands in last night?" If she was confused, then so was I. "At first, I thought you and Logan were going to hook up but then last night you were feeling Sammy up."

"You do remember I'm a lesbian, right?" She laughed at my expression. "I think those two are missing certain parts to hold my interest."

"I know," I quickly defended myself. To be honest, I hadn't seen her with another girl. No hand holding or anything. "Are you sure you're a lesbian?" I asked doubtfully.

She cocked her head at me, the words written all over her face.

"I just think you'd make a cute couple. Logan is really nice!" Since when did I become a match-maker?

"Logan," she emphasized, smirking at me, "is a man whore. He makes Mr. Grey look like a fucking saint!"

I laughed at her description. She hit it right on the head. I think I'd seen Logan with six different women since I'd been here.

"Besides..." She focused back on the book in her lap, looking nervous. "The girl I'm interested in isn't available. She's not into me like that."

I got up out of my seat, hating the anxiety written all over Bex's face. She was always such a cheery person and seeing her looking so defeated and withdrawn wasn't right. I wrapped my arms around her and pulled her sideways toward me until she was resting her head on my shoulder.

"Well, it's her loss! She doesn't deserve someone as amazing as you." Which was right. How could anyone not see how amazing Bex was? She was funny, smart, kind, fierce, loyal and if I was a lesbian, I'd be into Bex.

"Thanks." She chuckled, pulling away from me. "Anyway..." A smirk crept over her face making me cringe before the words even left her mouth. "What did you get up to last night?"

"Up to?" I retorted, painting an innocent mask over my face. "I don't know what you mean."

"Bullshit!" she shrieked, laughing.

Before I could move, she reached over, digging her

fingers into my ribs. I squealed, kicking my legs out and trying to escape her grip. She was a relentless tickler.

"Come, on!" she taunted. "Spill it! You had sex."

I hated being tickled. It set me off into fits of giggles until I had tears streaming down my cheeks.

"Fine!" I half-shrieked, half-yelled. "We did! We had sex!" I had wriggled so much that I had my legs over the arm of the sofa with my head in her lap. She removed her hands, smirking down at me triumphantly.

"How did it go?" she asked,

"I'm not giving you a play-by-play." I laughed up at her, feeling quite comfortable lying where I was.

"No." Her face cleared, giving me a small smile. "I mean, did it go okay? Was he gentle?"

I smiled back at her, loving how protective she was. I nodded, trying to choose the correct words. "He was really sweet." I smiled, thinking back on the previous night. It couldn't have been more perfect. The more I allowed the memories to flash through my mind, the more I could start to feel the tingles shooting through me.

"So, his performance was above average, then?" She gave me a cheeky wink making me flush.

I got up and walked to the doorway by the stairs before grabbing the cushion from the window seat and throwing it at Bex. "Well above average!" I shrieked before running up the stairs with Bex hot on my trail.

After the worst pillow fight ever with me failing to get my revenge for her tickling nightmare earlier on, Bex left, promising to message me later. Her parents were stopping by that night to visit her and had promised to take her out to dinner. She had yet to come out to them and she was trying to find the confidence to do so.

Grabbing my laptop, I lay down on my bed, facing away from the door. Swinging my legs in the air, I waited for the connection to go live. I hadn't spoken to my father all week. His face appeared on the screen, making me smile.

"Hi, Dad." I grinned at him, waving at the screen like an idiot.

"Hi, sweet girl." He grinned back, the laugh lines creasing by his eyes. "How has school been?"

"Good." I nodded my head. "I have a few projects due but overall, it's been good."

"I spoke to Joy during the week." He gave me that fatherly concerned look. "I hear there's a boy on the scene."

I was going to kill Joy. Before I could say a word, his expression moved, almost as if he was looking at something behind me. I turned, cringing when I saw Johnny in the door. I giggled when Johnny cringed.

"Yeah," I said, directing my words to my Dad. "Can we talk about it later?"

"Sure." He nodded, leaning back. "How about you call me later?"

"I will." I nodded my head, hating the turn the conversation had taken. "Love you, Dad."

"Love you, too, sugar." He grinned, disconnecting the call.

"I'm sorry," Johnny apologized.

"Don't be." I closed the laptop, getting up and placing it back on my desk. "He was going to find out soon." I went over to him, wrapping my arms around his waist. "You'll get to meet him at Christmas time."

"I may not be here." He cringed, looking down at me. "I usually go back and see my Mom at that time of year."

"Oh." I was disappointed. I'd just assumed—stupidly —that we would be spending Christmas together. Just thought his mom would come and see him instead of the other way around.

"I'm sorry, baby," he sighed, squeezing me to him.

"Don't be." I shook my head, looking up at him. "She's your mother. Of course you want to spend Christmas with her." I laid my head against his chest. "Moms are important."

He walked us forward, sitting down on the bed. Tapping his leg, he invited me to crawl into his lap and laying my head on his shoulder, I sighed as thoughts of Christmas with my own mother plagued my mind.

"You can talk to me about her," he whispered, rubbing his hand up and down my back before pressing a kiss to my forehead. "What was her favorite color?"

"She didn't have one." I chuckled, shaking my head. "If you asked her what her favorite color was, she would always say rainbow." I smiled, remembering how special she was. "Like that was a color."

"She sounds like an amazing lady," Johnny replied.

"She was." I wrapped my arms around his neck, gazing up at him. "She would have loved you."

"Yeah?"" He grinned down at me. "So, was she a football fan?"

"She was." I laughed, loving talking about her with him. My dad proposed to her at a football game. He was a footballer at college and she ran the merchandise stand. Her dad was the coach."

"No shit." He laughed down at me. "Love at first touchdown, then."

I laughed at his description. I guess that was exactly what it had been.

His eyes flicked down to my lips and then back to my eyes. I nodded, giving him the green light and moaned as he pressed his lips to mine. Ever since the night before, every time his lips had touched me, they had sent a direct signal to my core, almost as if it remembered exactly what Johnny could do to my body.

I thrust my tongue into his mouth, feeling a switch turn inside me. I had gone from meek and innocent virgin to horny student within twenty-four hours. I turned in his lap, placing my knees on the bed on either side of him. The position was a direct mirror of last night, which wasn't helping the situation.

He stood before turning us around and laying me down on the bed, his hips fitting perfectly in between my open legs. He thrust against me gently, his lust taking over.

I pulled my lips away, cringing at the contact.

"Sore?" he asked, tucking a stray curl behind my ear.

I nodded, hating that we were having this conversation.

"I'm sorry, baby." He rolled off me, running his hand through his hair and exhaling a deep breath.

"It's okay," I whispered. We were back to staring at the ceiling again. Just like last night before we'd had sex for the first time. It had been perfect, and I wouldn't change a thing. "Can we do... other stuff?"

He looked toward me. "Like what?"

I couldn't bring myself to look at him. How the hell did I, being my shy and geeky self, bring this up with the sex god that was lying next to me?

"Can I touch you?" I asked, turning on my side and placing my hand on his chest.

"You are." He rested his hand over mine, smiling down at me. There was a spark of confusion in his eyes. He didn't get it.

I moved my hand from beneath his, sliding it down over his toned stomach and dipping my fingers beneath the buckle of his jeans.

"Woah!" he grabbed my wrist, yanked my hand out of his trousers. "I, uh... I don't think..."

He was stammering. Was he nervous? Or did he not want me to touch him there? I had heard guys liked being touched there. My insecurity reared its ugly head.

"I just..." He puffed his chest out before taking a deep breath and blowing it out. "I am going to blow my load if you touch me there." His throat bobbed up and down several times.

He was nervous.

"I thought that was the point." I gave him a cheeky smile before leaning over and pressing my lips to his. He groaned, parting his. I kissed him harder, trying to take his mind off it.

"Did you like watching me come apart for you last night?" I asked, whispering the words in his ear.

"Fuck, yes." He pressed a kiss against my neck before sucking the skin. "Seeing you above me..."

"Did you like knowing that you were my first? That I had never been with anyone else?"

It wasn't like me to talk like this, but I wanted to do so for Johnny because of what he had done for me last night. I had never been put first like that—never had someone focus so much attention on me before. I wanted to make him feel as special as he had made me feel.

He nodded his head, no words following.

"This can be another first," I whispered. "Let me do this."

He groaned against the skin of my neck. He gently kissed up my neck until he got to my ear. He nibbled the lobe before soothing it with his tongue. I slid my hand down, grasping the button on his jeans before popping it open. He took hold of my wrist, rubbing his thumb over my pulse point.

"If it gets uncomfortable or you start to feel awkward, we can stop, okay?" His eyes were locked on mine, truth shining in them.

I nodded, secretly loving the way he was protective of me.

I slipped my hand inside, surprised when Johnny pulled his trousers and boxers down a little, freeing his dick from his pants. I was shocked he was so... so... big. I really wasn't expecting it. His dick bobbed a little, standing tall like a soldier. It didn't look as scary as I thought it would. It was just skin.

"Can I help?" he asked, taking hold of my hand.

I nodded, having no freaking clue what to do. Where did I start? Did he like soft and gentle? Or hard and fast?

He guided my hand to his firmness. It was surprisingly soft and hard all at the same time.

Gliding our hands up, I bit my lip at the texture of him.

He groaned, wrapping my hand tighter around his shaft. On the next pass, he pulled my hand further down to the base, squeezing tightly before pulling it back up to the top. Twisting my hand, I tried thinking back on all the hand job facts I had read about in teen mags over the years.

He groaned at the action, his head dropping backwards.

"Is that good?" I asked. It was a stupid question because obviously it was; I just needed to hear him.

"Yes, baby. Fuck that feels amazing." His hips rotated slowly before dropping back down. His hand fell away from mine, letting me take over.

I tightened my grip, squeezing the base. "Is it better than last night?" I was curious to know how it compared. Was the act of sex more intense because feelings were involved or was it just down to hormones?

"It's good, baby." He closed his eyes, his tongue peeking out to wet his lips. "But it doesn't..." He shook his head, groaning loudly when I slid my thumb over the slit at the head of his dick. "Fuck, it's nowhere near as good as your pussy."

My legs tensed at hearing his raw description of our love making. It was love making but hearing him talk so dirty and graphic about last night; it was hotter. More intense.

Why did I have to be sore?

Pumping him harder, I smiled when I started to see a creamy liquid begin to leak from the slit of the head. It didn't look horrible. I felt proud seeing it there and I had never felt sexier. I pumped him harder, my hand now flying up and down his shaft wanting... no... needing him to come apart. I needed to know what I did to him—needed to know that he desired me just as much as I desired him.

On my next pass, I trailed my other hand down and slid my pointer finger in between the crease of his balls. I had never given that part of Johnny much thought before, but I couldn't deny that seeing him in the throes of passion had left me curious. My finger had barely touched him when he started groaning louder and thrusting his hips up and down in time with my pumping actions.

He quickly lifted his shirt to his chest before moving my hand off him. He gave himself an extra few rough pumps before he ejaculated, the sperm landing on his stomach. Looking at the substance, I could see that it was a little thick and sticky. He took his shirt off, wiping it away. Rolling his shirt up, he tossed it on the floor.

His chest was heaving, and his eyes were shut tight. Watching him, I had never been so turned on. One night with Johnny and I had become a sex-crazed student.

"Fuck, baby." He opened his eyes, looking straight into mine. "Don't look at me like that."

"Like what?" I asked, whispering. I was so turned on that I just wanted to jump him right here.

"Like you want to eat me up." He licked his lips, his eyes darkening with want.

I bit my lip, trying to decide how to tell him that's exactly what I did want to do. Words weren't necessary, though. Before I could blink, Johnny grabbed my arms and yanked me down to his lips.

Words weren't necessary.

14

JOHNNY

THE WEEKS HAD SLOWLY PASSED UNTIL WE WERE only a few days from Christmas. Tillie and I had barely had any time together, mostly due to the amount of coursework we both had. Considering it was Tillie's first year, the professors weren't taking it easy on her. Every time I saw her on campus, she always had a sheet of notes in front of her or was sketching some ugly monstrosity of art. I could appreciate art as much as the next random person but what was the point in drawing a misshapen blob of clay. I shook my head, not understanding it.

Tillie's heart lay in landscapes and they should have been pushing her down that path. Next year, they would be merging teaching subjects with her practical art subjects. That's where her heart truly lay. She wanted to teach, and she'd be perfect at it. Plus, teaching would be perfect as she could do that anywhere. No matter where we were.

I shook my head, rolling my eyes at myself. What the

hell had happened to me? I was now considering a life plan with Tillie in it. I couldn't deny that she had me by the balls. I thought of her day and night. I wasn't sure if I loved her but... I thought about her a lot. Like all the time.

Was that love? Was having someone you constantly thought about day and night, love?

I shook my head, focusing back on the present in front of me. It was for Mom. I'd bought her our team jersey, a ball, some perfume and a pair of tickets to a game of her choosing.

Sticking a fake bow to the top, I sighed. I fucking hated wrapping presents.

Sammy walked in to the kitchen, grinning. "What's with the sulky face?"

"I'm not sulking." I grabbed the present, taking it into the lounge.

We leave for Christmas tomorrow. Tillie's present was wrapped and beneath the tree. It was tiny compared to everyone else's present but I knew she was going to love it. I just hated I wouldn't be with her over Christmas. Her father was traveling up to spend the holiday with her and Joy. It'd be a full house as some of Joy's relatives were traveling down to spend it with her as well.

A knock came from the front door, disturbing me from my thoughts. Opening it, I grinned when I saw it was Tillie. I guessed it would be the last time I'd see her until New Year's. She was bouncing on the spot with a red box in her arms and three smaller presents on top.

"Hi, baby." I took the presents off her, giving her a quick kiss.

"Merry Christmas."

I laughed when she took her hood down, seeing the sparkly red headband in her hair. The girl loved Christmas! It was good to see as I had caught her a few times a little low whenever she thought of her mother and I'd take bouncy Tillie any day of the week.

"The Christmas Nazi has arrived," Logan joked, coming down the stairs. His description was perfect. When we'd been putting up the decorations, she had demanded we needed red, green and gold on the tree as they were the Christmas colors. Apparently.

She poked her tongue out, not caring. "I just came over to wish you guys safe travels." She reached into the pouch of her hoodie and pulled a small box out. It was wrapped in gold paper and had a tiny silver ribbon bow on top. "This is for your mom." She handed it to me with a shy smile.

"You didn't have to do that." I took the box from her, pulling her into a hug. Rocking her from side to side, inhaling her fresh vanilla scent, I didn't want to let her go. If I'd been a bigger asshole, I'd have suggested blowing off our families and just spending it together.

"I'm going to miss you guys." She pulled back, her eyes filling with unshed tears. "Who's going to give me my daily insults?" she asked, looking toward Logan.

"I don't mind staying," Logan replied, shrugging his shoulders.

"No." Like fuck was I leaving that horn dog with my girl.

They both laughed, obviously knowing exactly what I was thinking. I know he wouldn't dare touch her, but I'd be jealous as hell.

"When does your dad get here?" I asked, pulling her toward the sofa. Taking a seat next to me, she kept her hand in mine.

"Oh." She looked down at the floor before sighing. "He's not coming." She shook her head, looking dejected. "One of the guys he works with has been given the time off instead. His wife has gone into labor, so my dad has to work over Christmas." She shrugged her shoulders trying to look strong, but she wasn't.

"I'm really sorry, Tillie," Logan said.

"It's not your fault, Logan." She smiled at him, acting as if it wouldn't ruin her first Christmas away from him.

I nodded my head toward the stairs, Logan getting the message as he jogged back up them.

"Come home with me," I whispered, playing with her fingers.

"What?" She turned her head to look at me.

"Come home with me," I repeated. "I don't want you here alone."

"I won't be." She shook her head. "I can't leave Joy."

"Joy has family coming to visit her. She's not going to be alone."

"What would your mother think if you took me home? She's probably looking forward to having you and Sammy all to herself." She laughed, trying to talk her out of herself.

"Seriously?" I cocked an eyebrow at her. "My mother is the craziest person I know. She's probably already setting a dinner place for you. Anyway, Logan is coming home with us aswell."

She frowned, looking confused. "He's not going home to his parents."

I shook my head. "Logan basically grew up around my house. Short story; his parents died when he was little, and he basically lived around mine. He was always welcome, and he just became a part of the family."

"Poor Logan," she whispered. "That must have been awful."

"So, come home with us. Trust me, you won't be intruding."

"I don't know." She nibbled her lip. "Let me go and talk to Joy."

I nodded, letting her escape. Joy would push her out the door. I grinned, jogging upstairs to finish packing. Things were looking better.

Hours later, we were on the road. Just me, Logan, Sammy and a sleeping Tillie. Her fingers were dusted with the smudge from her pink pastel. Tillie had had no clue what to get for Joy for Christmas, so she was working on a pastel flower sketch for her. She had become obsessed with flowers in her sketches lately and I was sure it was linked to Joy. She always referred to Tillie as 'flower'. I knew she was going to love it.

Chunk had let us borrow his car, yet again, with the promise that we wouldn't return straight away. Our house was no doubt going to become party central for the next few days and he didn't want a stupid, loved up couple getting in the way.

Pulling up outside the house, I chuckled when I saw the curtains move. Mom had probably been sitting by that window waiting all day long. Turning the engine off, I grabbed Tillie's hand, leaving Sammy and Logan to see mom first. I had never seen Tillie look so nervous.

"Relax." I pulled her hand to my lips, pressing small kisses to each of her fingers. "She will love you."

She took a deep breath, nodding her head determinedly.

Climbing out of the car, I grinned, opening my arms wide. Mom jumped into my arms, squeezing me around the middle.

"Look at you," she said, beaming up at me. "You've gotten so big." She pulled back, stepping a couple of paces away.

I laughed at her comment. "Yeah, the coach has been training us hard."

Tillie walked around the back of the car and I immediately held my arm out for her. Tucking her at my side, I smiled over at Mom. "Mom, this is Tillie. Tillie, this is my mother, Gill."

"Hi, Mrs. Baker." Tillie gave her a small awkward wave, shuffling her feet on the spot.

"Hello, sweetheart." Mom walked up to her and pulled her into a hug. "She's gorgeous," she mouthed to me over Tillie's shoulder. She pulled back, taking Tillie's arm in hers. "Let's go and get you settled." She began leading Tillie up the path before turning her head. "Fetch the bags, boys."

I grabbed Tillie's bag and my own, leaving the boys to sort their own luggage out. Tossing the keys to Sammy, I left him to lock up. I took the bags straight upstairs, wondering where Tillie would be staying. Every room was officially taken, and no way was she bunking with Sammy or Logan.

Walking back downstairs, I smiled when I saw Tillie sitting on the sofa. I sat next to her, taking her hand in mine.

"Your mom is really nice," she whispered.

I grinned, giving her a quick kiss just as mom walked back in the room.

"Aw, look at you guys." She smiled, carrying in a tray with five mugs. "I don't know how you did it, Tillie, but I thought Johnny would never settle down." She handed a hot chocolate to Tillie, leaving the coffees on the tray on the coffee table.

Logan and Sammy joined us, sitting on the floor on either side of Mom, grabbing a biscuit each and dunking it in their cups.

"Disgusting, isn't it?" Logan laughed, getting an elbow in the ribs from Mom.

"Thank you for letting me crash your Christmas, Mrs. Baker. My dad had to work and..." She shrugged her shoulders.

"Don't be silly. You're welcome, sweetie." She grinned at me before her eyes went back to Tillie. "It's nice to finally put a face to the name of the girl Johnny's been going on and on about."

I rolled my eyes. You'd swear there was a biological link between her and Logan. They were so much alike.

Tillie yawned, blushing when everyone stared. "Sorry." She giggled, setting her mug down on the table. "It's been a long day."

Sammy cleared the table, taking everyone's mugs out to the kitchen.

"So..." I cleared my throat. "What's the sleeping arrangements?" I hated to have this conversation so openly, but Tillie had to sleep somewhere.

"Tillie is welcome to stay in your room. But remember..." She pointed her finger at me with a kind of stern expression on her face. "My walls are thin."

I groaned, nodding my head. Taking Tillie's hand, I led her up the stairs after saying good night. My mom trusted me, but she sometimes had a big mouth.

She smiled, sitting on the edge of the bed. "Can I have your shirt?" Her eyes trailed down to my chest.

I grinned, pulling it off and held it out to her. Without any warning, she lifted her top off until she was standing in only her jeans and white, lace bra.

I groaned, adjusting myself. We'd only had sex once, but her confidence had grown loads in the last few weeks.

"You're testing me." I smirked down at her, watching her slip my tee over her head.

She smiled, inhaling the collar and letting her eyes drift closed for a few seconds. "I like smelling of you."

Watching her slide her jeans down her legs, I wanted nothing more than to christen my bed with her, but I never would with my mom in the house.

She climbed into bed, looking right at home. Doing a quick change, I slipped some basketball shorts on over my boxers and joined her in bed, turning the lights off as I did. Spooning her from behind, I sighed at the feeling that coursed through me.

Complete. Bliss.

This was where she belonged. Right there. In my arms.

Waking up the next day, I groaned when I saw Tillie wasn't there. Her side of the bed was cold, so she had obviously been up for a while. Climbing out of bed, I pulled a pair of sweats on and a black tee before brushing my teeth. Going downstairs, I laughed at the sight in front of me. Sammy and Logan were both on their phones, Mom was in the kitchen and Tillie was sitting by the tree. She was dressed in a red dress, white cropped leggings and a festive Santa hat.

It looked like everyone's presents had been separated into piles. This was a first. Usually everyone's presents were beneath the tree. I guess the Christmas Nazi had been unleashed.

She looked up, beaming at me. She jumped up from her spot, coming toward me. She wrapped her arms around me until she was in my arms, her feet dangling inches from the floor.

"You're looking very festive today." I laughed at her. She didn't care that people would think of her as strange. She was who she was, and nothing was going to change her.

She giggled before pressing her lips to mine and untangling herself from me. As she took her seat back by the tree, I wanted nothing more than to have her curled up on my lap but there was another lady I had to give my time to that day. She came in with a tray of five flutes of buck's fizz before everyone dived into their presents. We all wished each other a merry Christmas before taking our seats around the tree.

Tillie looked over, smiling at me. Sipping her flute, she turned to look at Sammy, laughing at the excited expression on his face. He'd gotten the new Yankee's jersey. Anyone would swear he had the winning lottery ticket in his hands instead.

A few presents later, Mom handed Tillie's present to me and nodded her head toward her. I grinned, moving closer to Tillie and handing her a small box wrapped in red paper.

She smiled at me before grabbing a medium sized box wrapped in gold from behind her.

"Open mine first." She held it out to me, fidgeting.

"Nervous, T?" Sammy asked.

"Very." She sat back, waving me on to unwrap it.

I ripped the paper off, revealing a red box. Opening it up, I took out a brown football, much like the one I used on the field. On the ball was the printed stamp of the NFL.

"Turn it over," she whispered.

I did just that, smiling at the badge imprint on the other side: #1—just like her jersey.

"I love it." I took her hand in mine, bringing it to my lips. "Now, it's your turn."

She grinned, unwrapping the small box. It was tiny, but I hoped the gift inside would mean as much to her as it did to me. She turned the small green box in her hands and flipped the lid. She gasped, her eyes filling with water.

"Johnny..." The tears spilled over her lids, leaving marks on her dress.

"We'll give you both some time." Sammy tapped me on the shoulder before the three of them left us alone.

"Turn it over," I whispered, repeating her words from earlier.

She did so, and I saw her bottom lip tremble in response. "Do you mean it?" she asked, lifting her head to look at me.

"Every word, baby." I held my hand out for hers and pulled her over to me. She sat across my lap, holding the box close to her. "You are my missing piece," I replied, repeating the words that were inscribed on the back of her necklace: a silver jigsaw piece.

I took it from her, fastening it around her neck. I smiled, loving the way it fell in the centre of her collarbones. She really was it. My missing piece. In every way.

"Thank you."

"You're welcome, baby." I pressed lips to hers, loving the way she melted against me.

THE NEXT DAY, we were all in the lounge watching some stupid cheesy film that Tillie had demanded we watch. Logan was snoring, and Sammy and Mom were cuddled up on the sofa. My phone rang with Joy's number. Excusing myself, I moved Tillie's legs off my lap, heading out the front door to take the call. I didn't like the dreaded feeling that filled my gut at seeing her name flash on the screen.

"Hello? Joy? Is everything okay?" I asked, firing all the questions at her.

"Hello, sweet boy," she replied, sounding okay. "How is your Christmas going?"

"Yeah, it's fine. Good to see Mom." Silence. "Is everything okay?"

"I feel so silly calling but..." She sounded worried.

"What is it?" I was starting to worry now and really needed her to talk faster.

"We have a little problem." She sounded apologetic.

"What kind of problem?" This didn't sound good.

"I just don't want Tillie to worry."

"Okay." I nodded before realizing she couldn't see me.

"I'm just calling to say..."

Before she could get any further, I was shocked from behind by Tillie.

"Johnny!" She yelled my name and then came shooting out the front door. She had tears streaming down her face and was holding her phone out to me.

"What's the matter?" I asked, holding my phone out.

"Joy. The hospital... she's in the hospital."

"What happened?" I asked, holding the phone back to my ear.

"This is silly," she mumbled before continuing. "I had a little fall and Chunk called an ambulance. I'm fine but they want to do more tests."

"Okay." I sighed, frustrated. Just when things were starting to look up. "One second. Here's Tillie."

She took the phone off me and started firing questions. "Are you okay? What happened? Why didn't you call me?" She ended with, "I'm coming home."

A few minutes later, she disconnected the call before

moulding herself to my chest. Looking up at me, her eyes filled with water. "I have to go home, Johnny."

She didn't want to, I could see it in her eyes, but Joy had taken Tillie into her home in her hour of need. They were family. Much like Mom and I were.

I nodded, before leading her inside.

15

TILLIE

Sitting next to Johnny in the car, I wanted to cry. I hated pulling him away from Christmas with his mother. Sammy and Logan had decided to stay and spend the rest of the time with her and would catch the train back.

"I'm so sorry, Johnny," I apologized for the thousandth time.

"Stop apologizing." He took my hand before bringing it to his lips. He pressed soft kisses to the back of it before resting our clasped hands on his leg. "She's family. Mom understands that."

I smiled, loving the feeling of warmth that spread up my arm from his touch.

When we told Gill about Joy's fall, she basically packed my bag for me telling me that family comes first. Before we left, she squeezed me so hard I thought I was going to bust. I had come to love Gill's hugs. She made you feel so loved with just one hug. It reminded me a lot of my own mother.

I gazed up at Johnny, my fingers gently rubbing his leg. He looked at me from the corner of his eyes before smirking.

Fuck, he was sexy.

"Baby, you need to stop that." He tried looking stern but the twinkle in his eye gave him away.

"Stop what?" I asked, rubbing my fingers harder against his leg and inching further upwards.

"If you don't stop..." His hand grabbed my wrist, stopping my movements. "I will be pulling over and christening that back seat with you."

I giggled, imagining him doing just that. We hadn't been intimate since my sloppy hand job before Christmas.

"Maybe I want you to," I teased, whispering in his ear.

He groaned, his pants starting to get tight. "If I didn't know who else had christened that back seat, you'd already be back there."

I wrinkled my nose in disgust, pulling my hand away. "Fair enough."

No way was I doing anything sexy with Johnny anywhere near where Chunk might have done it.

We arrived back in town but went straight to the hospital. I followed Johnny to the correct ward and we were quickly shown to Joy's room. Johnny walked in with me behind. I hated hospitals. Ever since I was little, I'd classed hospitals as the place death came.

"Hi, sweet boy," Joy greeted, accepting a hug off him. It was like watching a giant hug a smurf.

"I've brought a surprise for you." He stepped aside so that Joy could see me.

I wanted to cry when my eyes met hers. She had bruises all over her face. I burst into tears and went straight to her. Within minutes, my feet were off the floor and I was sobbing into her chest. I couldn't lose Joy. She had slowly filled the large hole that my mother had left behind.

"Hush now," she whispered, gently smoothing the hair away from her face. "It's okay."

After a few minutes, my sobs subsided leaving me to inhale her fresh vanilla scent. I loved the way that she always smelled like summer. My eyes went to Chunk when he walked in, giving him a small wave. He grinned, responding with that cheeky wink that he always gave me. He looked at Johnny, nodding his head toward the hallway.

Johnny nodded, quickly following and leaving Joy and I alone.

"How did your Christmas go, sweet girl?" she asked, rubbing my back.

"It was good." I tilted my head to look up at her. "I met Johnny's mom."

"And how did that go?"

"Good." I nodded my head. "I think she liked me." I was pretty sure that she did.

Before we left, she'd asked Johnny to go for a walk with her. He came back looking a little flustered. I wasn't sure if it was from the cold or not, but Gill looked so happy. Maybe it was something she had wanted to say to him and was now relieved that she had. He never brought it up and I never asked. I guessed he'd tell me if and when he was ready.

"Munchkin!" Chunk greeted me when he came in. "How about you and I go and get something sugary for Joy? This hospital food is crap and I say she needs some perking up."

I nodded, pressing a quick kiss to Joy's cheek before leaving her with Johnny. We took extra-long as Chunk couldn't decide between pink iced donuts or whether she'd prefer plain glazed ones. I didn't think I had ever met anyone who put as much thought into sugary products as he did.

Walking back in, I noticed that Joy had a flush on her cheeks. She kept grinning at Johnny strangely. I wasn't sure what that was about.

"Is everything okay?" I asked, looking between them.

"Of course." Johnny cleared his throat. He looked nervous for some reason. "Just talking about the next season."

I nodded my head, playing along. Whatever it was, he didn't want to tell me.

"Stop fussing, missy," Joy chirped in, smirking at me. "Now give me those donuts and you two go home and get settled."

I nodded, placing the donuts on her bedside table, giggling at Chunk who couldn't stop staring at them.

Arriving back home, I dragged my bag into Johnny's, feeling too lazy to go home and unpack it just yet. I just wanted to crash. It had been such a long day. Johnny must have been more tired than I was from all that he'd done. He took my hand and began leading me up the stairs. I guessed he had the same idea.

I followed him into his room. His bed looked so comfy and I knew it was going to knock me right out. I turned to shut the door and the second it clicked shut, I was jolted from behind me. I gasped when I felt Johnny press himself against me, trapping me against the door.

"I have thought of nothing but being alone with you all week," he growled. His lips quickly descended to my neck where he began to lick, kiss and suck my skin.

I groaned, arching my back and tilting my hips, rotating my ass cheeks against his erection. I could feel how turned on he was, and it was making me horny as hell. Considering we had only had sex once, it hadn't dampened down how much I wanted him. Our first time had been slow and gentle. Judging by how roughly he was kissing my neck and holding my hips to his, I had a feeling this was not going to be soft or gentle.

"You want me..." I gasped as he thrust himself harder against my ass. His teeth sunk in to the column of my neck, making me moan.

"I always fucking want you." His hand fisted in the back of my hair before pulling my face to his. He thrust his tongue into my mouth, sucking my tongue into his. "You have bewitched me." He spun me around before lifting me up by my ass and grinding his jean-clad erection against my open legs. He held me against the door with his hips before grabbing the hem of my top and ripping it upwards. His lips quickly descended, sucking the tops of my breasts.

I groaned, grabbing his top and pulling it upwards. He pressed his chest against mine, making goose bumps spread all over my skin. His head dropped back to my neck, locking my legs behind him.

"I just want to fuck you so bad." He groaned, reaching his hands up and roughly grabbing my bra-clad breasts.

"Do it," I gasped, tilting my head backwards. Having his hands on my skin sent me into pure bliss.

He froze, pulling back a little to look into my eyes.

"If you're sure..."

I nodded, needing him. I had never been a highly sexual person but being with Johnny was different. I felt different when I was with him. He was it for me and I never wanted it to stop. I tightened my legs around him, holding on as he walked us over to his bed.

He lowered me to the floor, looking at me with hunger. His fingers went to the button on my jeans, undoing it. I kicked my flats off before he lowered himself down, sliding my jeans down my legs as he went.

I placed my hands on his shoulders, leaning on him for support. Sitting down on his bed dressed in only my white bra and panties, my eyes followed him as he stood back up. I lifted my hand, intending to do the same for him but he quickly stepped back, his Adam's apple bobbing. That was always a nervous habit of Johnny's, but he had nothing to be nervous about.

He tossed his jeans on top of mine and I gasped when I realized he had been going commando. I rubbed my legs together, feeling the tingles shoot straight to my core. He leaned over me, pressing me back so that I was lying sideways on the bed. His hands gripped the elastic at my hips and pulled it down. He tossed it on our discarded pile of clothes before picking me up and laying me down the right way so that my head was on his pillow.

Seconds later, he was joining me. It was different from last time. This time he was the one on top of me, his erection trapped between us.

"If you want to stop..." He tucked some loose curls behind my ears before softly kissing the tip of my nose. "We'll stop. Okay?"

I nodded, spreading my legs wider for him. The thing I had come to learn about Johnny was that he would only do what I wanted. If I didn't want something, that'd be enough for him. If he was going to be rough with me, I would have to initiate it. I slid my hands down his back, loving the shiver that rippled through him. Grabbing his ass cheeks, I roughly pushed him down against me.

"I want you to fuck me," I whispered in his ear before turning my head and licking up the column of his neck and nibbling his earlobe.

He groaned, pushing his hips forward.

In one swift movement, he was deep inside me. I gasped at the feel of him inside me. Before I could get used to the feel of him, he began rocking his hips back and forward. Not slow or gentle. He had one hand settled on my ass and the other was massaging my breast. Even though it was covered by my bra, it didn't lessen the desire that was coursing through me from the actions.

He lifted himself up on his hands and began moving faster.

"Feel good?" he gasped, circling hips in between hard thrusts.

"Yes." I moaned, my hands leaning up to press against his chest. "You feel... so good."

"You like that? You like watching me fuck you?"

Fucking hell. Johnny's dirty talk was going to be the end of me.

"You like knowing how much of me you own? You like it when my rock-hard cock is inside you, fucking your sweet pussy?" He grinned down at me, knowing exactly the effect he had on me.

I slipped my hand over my mouth, trying to contain the noises that were coming from me.

"No, no, baby." He pulled my hand away, moving it back to his shoulder. "I want to hear you. No one is here. I want to hear you fucking scream." He leaned his weight down on me further, our chests pressing together.

I could feel him start to grow harder inside me, if that was possible. His hips sped up causing his head board to lightly hit the wall. I pulled his head down to mine, needing to feel as much of him as I could. He thrust his tongue inside, imitating what his hips were currently doing.

I moaned, ripping my lips from his. I could feel myself start to come undone.

"I...I'm.. I think I'm going to... Oh, fuck, Johnny!"

His hips sped up, determined to draw it out of me.

"That's it, baby girl. Come for me." He continued thrusting, my legs tightening around his hips. "Come apart for me!"

Within seconds, I was moaning out loud, thankful no

one else was in the house. It was neither quiet nor something I wanted anyone to hear. Several thrusts later, he groaned into my neck, collapsing some of his weight onto me as he came inside me. Minutes later, he began to pull back, lifting his weight off me.

"Don't go yet," I whispered, tightening my arms and legs around him. I was clinging to him like a monkey, but I didn't care. Feeling his skin against mine made me feel warm inside.

He dropped his head, pressing a small kiss to my shoulder.

"Tillie," he whispered. "Thank you."

"For what?" What could I possibly have done to deserve a thank you?

"For this. Being with me. Accepting me as I am." He turned his head, pressing his lips softly to mine. He pulled back, rubbing his nose against mine. He stared into my eyes, making me nervous. "Tillie Jacobs, I think I'm in love with you."

I froze at his words. In love? Was he serious? Did he feel everything that I felt? Did I plague his thoughts as much as he plagued mine? He had quickly become everything to me and I was so scared to allow myself to fall over that ledge with him—scared he wouldn't catch me, that I would plummet to the shore below and get washed out.

"I know it's early and..." He shook his head, unable to hide the look of disappointment. "I know I'm rushing it but..."

I couldn't stand it any longer. If he was in this for the long haul, then so was I. He began to lift his weight off me, but I forced him back, taking his face in my hands.

"I think I love you too," I whispered. "I know that's not the most romantic thing, but I have nothing else to compare it to." I smoothed his hair back, loving the way his green eyes filled with warmth. "You're all I think about and even when we're not together, you're on my mind. You're my missing piece, Johnny."

He grinned, apparently liking the idea of me repeating those inscribed words back to him.

From that moment on, we became inseparable. We had spent most of our time together before but since hearing Johnny tell me that he loved me, it just seemed to cement our connection further. Over the next few days, we spent our time between spending our evenings together and visiting Joy in the hospital. Johnny was focusing on getting as many of his essays completed as possible before college would start back up in the New Year.

Hanging out at the hospital had become my norm. I spent my nights at Johnny's and my afternoons with Johnny. In the mornings, I would spend the time catching up on my essays and cleaning the house. Joy was house-proud, and I didn't want her to be disappointed when she came home.

"So," Joy said, "What are you doing tonight?"

"Tonight?" I was confused. "Nothing that I can think of." I shrugged my shoulders, dismissively.

"Tillie!" she admonished me, sounding appalled. "It's New Year's Eve."

I laughed at how disgusted she sounded. "It's just

another night, Joy." I chuckled at the way she rolled her eyes. "I haven't celebrated New Year's Eve for a few years."

"Since losing your mama?" she asked, concerned.

I shrugged, not sure how to answer that. It's not like we never celebrated because of her, but it usually just ended with my nose in a sketchpad and my dad falling asleep in the chair.

"Well, you're not staying here." She had a fake stern expression on her face but her cheeky smile gave her away. "There's an outfit waiting at home for you and a party with Johnny that you will be at, young lady."

"Parties are not really my thing." I hated hanging out with large groups of people that I didn't really know. "Besides, you're here. Who's going to make me go?" I giggled at the flustered expression before we were interrupted.

"Knock, knock," a voice called from the doorway. "Reporting for Tillie duty."

I looked up and grinned. Logan and Sammy were both standing there with matching grins on their faces. Sammy had a box of chocolates in his hands and Logan was holding a pink 'Get Well Soon' balloon. They both greeted her with hugs and kisses. None of her blood relatives had visited as they had only come to visit for Christmas Day, but she still had us.

I disappeared into my sketch pad, trying to capture details from my mind for my animation subject. I fucking hated animation. I didn't have the imagination for it and it was stupid that I had to jump through this hoop just to pass the damned course.

After a few moments of feeling someone watching me, I flicked my eyes up.

Logan stood to the side of me, smirking down at me with his arms crossed. "You ready?"

Before I could even answer, he ripped the sketch pad from my lap and cocked an eyebrow at me, his eyes flicking between the sketch and me.

"Why are you drawing freaking unicorns?"

See? Even he thought it was stupid. I snatched it back, shoving my sketch pad back in my bag.

"Stop winding her up, bro." Sammy slung his arm over my shoulder giving me a wink.

"She knows I'm teasing, man." He grinned, bending down and giving Joy a quick kiss goodbye.

I gave her a tight hug, promising to come back and see her the next day. "Love you."

"Love you, too, sweet girl." She waved us off, smiling at us as we left.

16

JOHNNY

STANDING BY THE BUFFET TABLE IN THE HALL OF THE art museum in town, my eyes kept going to the door.

Fucking hell.

Another party. Another night. Another bimbo blonde giving me the 'come hither' look. I rolled my eyes, ignoring it. Avoiding Lucy's stare, I looked at Chunk, trying his hardest to hit on one of the sorority sisters. He didn't have a chance in hell. They only went for guys from rich families.

"Hi, Johnny," her nasal, annoying voice said from beside me. "It's good to see you." She reached over, grabbing my tie and used it to pull herself toward me. "Especially tonight." She licked her lips, attempting to look sexy. Several months ago, it would have worked.

"Hello, Lucy." I placed my arms on her upper arms, gently pushing her back away from me. The last thing I needed was for Tillie to walk in and see Lucy touching me. "Just waiting for Tillie."

"Still with that bitch?" she asked, her lip curling in disgust. "She can't satisfy you like I can."

"She satisfies me, just fine. Thank you for asking." I fucking hated Lucy. She may have been pretty on the outside, but she was ugly as sin on the inside. "Especially with her mouth."

She made a noise of disgust before turning around and stomping away. I didn't know why she hadn't just given up and moved on to the next poor fucker waiting in line.

I spent the next hour talking shit with Logan and the boys. He was asking a load of questions about game statistics and when he could expect to play. He just wanted one game. I guessed it'd be out of his system then.

"Hey, can I have some?" Bex asked, taking the bottle from Logan. She was dressed in a long, strapless black dress. Logan's eyes went straight to her chest. I felt for the poor guy. He obviously had yet to figure out that she wasn't into him; never would be if Tillie was correct.

"So, where's Tillie?" I asked, beginning to lose my patience. I was a patient guy but waiting over an hour was starting to make me frustrated.

"See for yourself." She nodded her head toward the door.

I followed her line of sight and gasped at the vision that stood before me. She was dressed in a cream dress that came to her knees. The bodice was lace and hugged her curves perfectly, but the bottom was frilly. She looked like a fairy. Her hair was curled and flowing down her back and she had the sexiest, matching cream heels on her feet. Tillie was never one for getting dolled up, but I could tell she had made the extra effort. My feet took me straight to her.

"You look beautiful," I whispered, leaning down and pressing my lips to hers.

"Thank you." She tucked some hair behind her ears before smiling shyly up at me. "Everyone's staring." Her eyes moved behind me, flicking around before coming back to mine.

"Ignore them." I took her hand in mine and began leading her to our table. She took her seat in between Sammy and me. I chuckled as she turned her body toward him. She fixed his tie, straightening it for him.

Looking around, I could see that half of the town was here. It was nice to be at an event that wasn't specifically just for college students.

"Would you like to dance, Tillie?" Sammy asked, holding his hand out for hers. She quickly accepted, letting him lead her to the dance floor. Sammy turned her so that her back was to us before Logan and Bex both turned to me at the exact same time.

"Where is it?"

"When are you going to do it?" They both fired off questions at the same time, making my head spin.

"Woah!" I raised my hands, trying to act cool. "What are you two on about?"

"Please!" Bex replied with attitude. "Sammy already told me!" She leaned closer to me, whispering. "You're going to ask Tillie to move in with you."

I looked at her in shock. How the fuck did she know what I was going to do? Shit! Did Tillie know?

I was starting to panic. I didn't know why the fuck I

was carrying the box around with her key tucked safely inside everywhere I went. I tried going over ideas in my head. It was all I'd thought about lately. I just didn't know how to ask her. I wanted it to be unique and special, but nothing seemed to pop out at me. It had gotten to the point that anytime we got close or made love, I'd have to undress myself, fearing that she'd find it. It wasn't like I was ready to settle down or anything, but I just knew, this key belonged to her. I belonged to her.

"Relax! You're starting to stress me out."

I couldn't stop staring at her. Sammy was twirling her beneath the sparkly lights and she looked like an angel. She tipped her head back, laughing at whatever Sammy was saying. Living without a father around, it was hard, but I had kind of become that figure to Sammy. Watching the two most important people in my world laugh together in that moment, it was right.

"May I cut in?" I asked, directing my question at Sammy.

He lifted her hand to his lips, pressing a soft kiss there before leaving the two of us.

She wound her arms around my neck, pressing her tiny body to mine. "You look very handsome," she said, her eyes flicking down to my suit jacket.

I hated dressing in monkey suits, but if it got her to look at me like that, then it didn't matter. I'd wear them every day. "Well, it is our first New Year's together, and I wanted to make it special." I smiled down at her, loving the way her eyes twinkled up at me.

"First? You planning for more?" She gave me a cheeky wink, but I understood the question.

"Many more." I bent my head, slowly pressing my lips to hers before pulling back.

After many more dances, I took her hand in mine and led her outside. We had only thirty minutes until midnight and I wanted this to be done before then. I'd been a nervous fucking wreck all night and I just wanted to get it over with. Walking through the gardens, she smiled at all the twinkly lights that were spread around us. If I hadn't known any better, I would have said it looked like the simple fantasy of heaven.

Technically it was. I had my angel right here with me. Life was looking pretty good.

I tightened my grip in hers, pulling her into my arms. As I rocked my hips from side to side, we slowly danced in a circle. Just the two of us. Surrounded by the lights. The moment was as perfect as it was going to get.

"Tillie," I whispered against her hairline.

She smelled beautiful: a mix of strawberries and vanilla. Bringing her lips up to mine, I gave her a quick kiss.

I smiled when I saw the faint dusting of pink chalk on her fingertips. I chuckled, imagining her doing some last-minute drawing in her frock before she came here.

She blushed, pulling her hand away, embarrassed that I had seen it. "I was surprised by tonight," she whispered, allowing me to hold her hand, placing it against my chest.

"You were?"

"I was." She nodded her head. "I kind of expected another college party." She frowned, collecting her thoughts. "Either that or for it to just be you and me."

"It's just me and you now." I smiled down at her. The nerves were creeping back up my spine, causing my feet to twitch.

"Are you okay?" She stroked the hair from my eyes with her other hand. "You look nervous."

I took a deep breath before nodding. "I'm so fucking nervous." I chuckled, trying to lighten the mood.

"Talk to me," she whispered. "What's wrong?"

"Nothing." I shook my head. "Everything is perfect."

The frown on her forehead creased. I was just confusing her more. I removed her hand from my chest and took a step back from her. It was now or never. Her hands dropped at her side before a look of hurt crossed her face.

I took her left hand in mine, needing this moment to be perfect.

"Before you, Tillie, I didn't know what I was doing. I didn't know that I was missing such a huge part of my life. College parties and sleeping around was just how it was supposed to be." I shrugged my shoulders, disappointed that I'd thought that. "But then, this crazy, strange, quiet girl moved in across the street from me. She tilted my axis and suddenly my whole word seemed to re-align. What was down was now up. I could suddenly see what was right in front of me."

Her eyes filled with tears before they slowly spilled over her cheeks.

"Tillie Jacobs." I took a deep breath before continuing. "I would love to share my home with you. For you to be mine completely. Mine to love. Mine to adore. Mine to protect." I dipped my hand into my trouser pocket. I opened the small blue box and held it open to her. "Will you move in with me?"

"Johnny, it's too soon." She shook her head, staring at the key nestled inside the box, shocked. "We've only been together a few months and we haven't really had any problems yet and I..." She was rambling now.

"Tillie." I took her left hand again, holding it tightly in mine. "Do you love me?"

"Of course I do, but..."

"Do you see yourself loving anyone else? The way that I love you?"

"No." It came out as a squeak due to how choked up she was. "But what if..."

"I love you. I will always love you. What else is there to know?"

She fidgeted, her fingers tightening around mine.

"Move in with me, Tillie."

Before I could say anything else, she nodded her head.

"Is that a yes?" I choked out the words, needing to hear her.

"Yes!" She giggled, wiping her tears away. "Yes, I'll move in with you."

I grinned, jumping to my feet. I picked her up, letting her wrap her arms around my shoulders and spun her around on the spot. Pressing my lips to hers, I kissed her, pouring as much of the passion coursing through me into it. Placing her down back on her feet, I grinned, loving the way she squeezed the key in between her fingers.

She grinned, looking down at it.

I pulled her to me, hugging her tight. Rocking her

there from side to side, life was blissfully perfect. Nothing could ruin it.

A shiver ran through her and she tightened her arms around my back, hugging me tight beneath my jacket.

"Let's go back in." I hugged her close, taking her back inside.

Walking back in, we headed straight for the bar. I could get served in most places whereas Tillie would still pass as a high school student due to her height. Ordering myself a quick beer and Tillie a fruity cocktail, we rejoined our table. We spent the build-up to midnight just chatting and Tillie laying her head on my shoulder.

When it was a few minutes to midnight, Tillie stood up and sat across my lap. She hung her arms around my shoulders, smiling up at me.

Tonight went perfectly. My girl looked happy as she stared up at me.

"You happy?" I asked, rubbing my nose against hers.

"So happy." She leaned up to press her lips to mine, but I pulled my head back.

"You can't kiss me yet," I teased. "It's not midnight."

She pursed her lips in the sexiest pout, turning those Bambi eyes on me.

The countdown started, resulting in everyone getting to their feet. Logan and Sammy were both holding one of Bex's hands each. That was an odd love triangle, if I could even call it that. What do you call something when two straight boys are both crushing on a very lesbian female?!

The countdown got down to a few seconds when I grasped Tillie's chin between my forefinger and thumb, slowly pulling her lips down to mine. I didn't want to roughly kiss her, not after tonight. I wanted to treat her like the angel that she was.

She grinned against my lips before pressing them firmly against mine. I groaned, loving the feel of her in my arms. I could kiss this girl forever and never get bored.

Sounds of celebrations and excitement erupted around us but it didn't stop us. We were in our own blissful bubble, just the two of us.

She pulled back, resting her forehead against mine. "Love you," she whispered.

"Love you too, baby," I whispered back.

She leaned up to give me a quick kiss before excusing herself to the ladies.

I grinned watching her go. When she disappeared out of sight around the corner, I froze as a hand settled on my shoulder and rubbed down over my chest.

"Hello, lover," Lucy purred, pressing her nose against my skin.

"Get off me!" I pulled my head away from her, not wanting her to be anywhere near me.

"Does she know?" she asked, walking until she was in front of me. Sitting in Tillie's chair, she smirked cockily. "Does she know that before you were fucking her..." She licked her lips, trying to look sexy. "That you were fucking me?" She slid her hand over my leg, climbing higher.

I grabbed her wrist, roughly shoving it away. "Keep your nasty mouth shut!"

I was angry. She thought she could hold this over my head, and the sad thing was, she could. This was going to break Tillie. She had asked me point blank if I had a sexual history with Lucy and I fucking lied.

"See you later." She smirked, standing up and leaving me.

The night was perfect, and it was quickly going to shit. If Lucy had her way, my days with Tillie were numbered. Lucy wouldn't stop. She was determined to win this game.

Minutes later, Tillie came bouncing back to the table, entwining her fingers with mine. "Do you want to get up and have a dance?" she asked.

"Sure." I smiled, trying to act nonchalant. Taking her hand, I led her to the dance floor just in time for the start of a new song. Several couples joined us as I began to gently sway Tillie from side to side. I rested my chin on the top of her head, trying to figure out how the fuck I was going to fix this clusterfuck.

"You okay?" Tillie asked, looking up at me. "You've gone really quiet."

"Just tired, baby." I pressed my lips quickly to hers before pulling back. "How about we go home?"

She yawned as soon as I finished asking her, making me chuckle.

"Let's get you home." I wound my arm around her, steering her to the door where Sammy was waiting. "Want to share a taxi?" I asked, directing my words at Sammy.

He nodded, looking just as dog-tired as Tillie. He wobbled to the side, obviously drunk.

"Where's Logan?" Tillie asked, looking around for him.

"Gone home with a friend." Sammy used quotation marks, rolling his eyes.

Tillie giggled, taking Sammy's hand in her free one. Bex ran ahead and opened the car door for us, before waving us off. As soon as we got in the car, he leaned his head on Tillie's shoulder, his eyes drifting closed.

Getting out of the taxi, Tillie held the door open for me. I grabbed Sammy by his arm, pulling his drunken ass out of the car. Tillie jogged ahead, unlocking the door with her brand-new key. Her smile was beaming as I passed her.

"I won't be long." I held his arm over my shoulders and began helping him up the stairs.

Tillie followed us up after locking the door and made her way into my room: soon to be ours.

Laying Sammy down on his bed, I pulled his shoes off, followed by his jeans. I pushed him backwards and flung the blanket on him. Poor fucker would be hungover in the morning.

Turning his light off, I walked in to my room to find Tillie waiting for me. She was lying in the centre of my bed, her head on my pillow dressed in her tank top and shorts pyjamas. It may have been winter, but Tillie always got too warm in the night.

I walked to the window, feeling drained. Right now, I should be cuddled up with her in that bed but all I could think about was Lucy and the words she'd said to me earlier. I knew that whatever she had planned wasn't going to be pretty.

I looked at Tillie, scared to death that our happy relationship was going to hit a major speed bump. I just hoped we would survive it.

Stripping out of my clothes, I kept my boxers on and climbed in behind Tillie. Wrapping my arms around her, I tried turning off my mind. Closing my eyes, I willed my body to relax. It didn't work. I tossed and turned all night long with one question constantly turning in my mind.

Was Lucy going to break Tillie's heart, or would I?

17

TILLIE

Walking to college, I groaned at the feel of the biting cold against my cheeks. I was wrapped up with my scarf, hat and gloves that Joy had given me before Christmas. She was due to come home today. I was excited to get her home.

Johnny and I had agreed to wait until Joy was back on her feet before breaking the news to her. I was excited to move in with the boys. Logan and Sammy had become like family to me. It was just Chunk I hadn't fully connected with, but I guess that would come with time.

Moving across campus, I was shocked to see Bex walk over to Lucy and her friends. That was new. As far as I knew, Bex hated them. I stood beneath one of the trees, trying not to make it obvious that I was gawking. Lucy stood up before Bex could get to her. They spoke for a few minutes before Bex shoved her finger in Lucy's face before walking away.

What the hell was that about?

Lucy re-joined her friends, laughing loudly. What-ever it was that Bex had said to her, she hadn't seemed to care.

I was determined to catch up to Bex later and to find out what that was about.

Hours later, I entered the cafeteria where I was hoping to catch up with her but for the first time, she wasn't in her usual spot.

Sitting next to Johnny, peeling my orange, my eyes kept going over to Bex's table, but there was still no sign of her.

"Everything okay?" Johnny asked, rubbing my leg.

"Just looking for Bex. I need to talk to her." I frowned, sucking on a piece of the juicy fruit.

"What's the problem? She okay?" he asked, concerned.

"I don't know." I shook my head. "I saw her this morning talking with Lucy and it didn't look like a happy conversation." I shrugged my shoulders, feeling defeated. My eyes went to Lucy, watching the way she laughed amongst all her followers.

"I thought she didn't like her."

See? Even he knew how much they hated each other. There is no reason why Bex should have been talking to her unless Lucy had done something to Bex.

"Do you think I should ask Lucy what's going on?"

"No!" Johnny, Sammy and Chunk yelled, making me jump.

"I don't want you anywhere near that poisonous bitch." Johnny seethed, taking my hand in his and resting it on top of the table. "She's a nasty piece of work."

220

I nodded, dropping the subject. One of my class-mates waved me over, with a piece of paper in his hand. I shrugged Johnny's arm off gently and headed over to him. Apparently, there was an art show we could submit animation pieces to. It wasn't my thing, but he seemed super excited about it.

I left him to get to class and made my way back over to Johnny. I froze in my tracks, shocked when Sammy raised his voice at Johnny.

"What the fuck! How could you have not said anything?" He sounded angry and looked a little red in the face.

"Keep your voice down!" Johnny snapped. "I don't need you making this shit any worse?"

"Is everything okay?" I asked, moving to stand next to Johnny. I looked between Johnny and Sammy waiting for an answer.

Johnny cocked his eyebrow at Sammy, waiting.

"It's nothing." Sammy's tense shoulders drooped before leaving. "See you later." He marched off, never looking back.

Johnny smiled down at me, taking my hand in his and leading me toward my next class. I wouldn't see him until that night due to his practice schedule.

"Come and see us later?" I asked, giving him a quick kiss.

He winked, leaving me to go in.

My eyes went straight to Bex's chair. It was empty. It was her favorite class and she wasn't there. Bex and Sammy were now both acting strange.

I shrugged my shoulders, taking my seat. I was determined to focus on this stupid subject. I was crap at the practical side of animation, but I hoped my theory essays would get me through it. After a lot of note taking, the class finally ended.

I left campus, not having the time to worry about it, and, checking my phone, I saw I had a text from Joy. She had arrived home from hospital. Damn it! I had wanted to be the one to take her home. Due to no car though, I guess it had been safer for her to get the ambulance drivers to do it.

I ran most of the way home, excited to see Joy back home where she belonged. Running through the door, I laughed at the smell that wafted through the house. She probably hadn't been home long, and I could already smell cookies baking.

I dropped my bag at the bottom of the stairs and headed toward the kitchen, but I froze when I got near the doorway.

"How do I tell her?" Bex whispered, her voice breaking. "I can't hurt her, Joy."

"Sweetie," Joy replied, sounding concerned. "You're hurting her by not telling her."

I couldn't take it any longer. I hated secrets and right then, one of the most important people in my world was keeping something from me. Secrets destroyed. There was a reason people kept them, right?

I moved into the doorway, surprising them both. Joy moved to leave the kitchen, but I shook my head.

"You can stay, Joy." My voice sounded strong, but inside I could feel my walls beginning to crumble. Bex had a look of devastation on her face that I knew was going to break me. I just hoped it wasn't going to break the both of us. "Where were you today?" I asked, directing my question to Bex. "Why weren't you in class? I looked for you at lunch. Where were you?"

She turned to me, taking a deep breath. "Don't hate me for what I'm about to say." Her eyes filled with tears.

"Why would I hate you?" I choked out. I tried swallowing past the lump in my throat, but it didn't work.

"I was hanging out with some junior students last night." She cleared her throat before continuing. "We got talking and... uh..." She looked away, staring at the floor.

"Just tell me, Bex. Whatever it is, we can get through it." I tried to be supportive, but I just really needed her to tell me whatever it was that was bothering her.

"A few of them said that Lucy was a bit of a whore."

Seriously? That's what we were talking about? Lucy and her sluttish behavior. I shook my head, confused.

"She slept with Johnny," Bex blurted out, freezing me.

As soon as the words were out, my blood ran cold. "They're lying," I replied. Why would people spread such bullshit? "Johnny and I already talked about this. Nothing ever happened between them."

"He lied to you, Tillie." She looked at Joy, defeated. "He's been lying to you from the start."

I shook my head, not believing her. "No! He wouldn't. You're lying."

"Why would I lie to you?" she defended, stepping closer to me. She took hold of my wrists, pulling me closer to her. "You are my very best friend and I would never do anything to hurt you!"

223

"Well you are!" I shrieked, pulling my hands from hers. "He would never lie to me! He loves me!" Tears leaked over my eyes and I wiped them away roughly. "We're going to move in together!" I yelled. "He wouldn't... he wouldn't do this to me." I was sobbing now, and I hated it. I shook my head, turning around and walking away.

"Sweet girl, where are you going?" Joy asked from behind me.

"To get some answers," I sobbed, leaving the house.

I ran toward the field, needing to calm myself down. It wasn't true. The quicker I spoke to Johnny, the better it would be. Walking into the arena, I spotted Sammy and Logan talking on the bench. Sammy turned toward me. He looked tense, but he still gave me a wave. I waved back hesitantly, keeping my very cold hands in my hoodie pocket.

Johnny looked over, grinning when he saw me. He wasn't wearing his helmet today. They seemed to be split into groups and working on catching the ball. Jogging over to me, he bent down to give me a kiss, but I couldn't.

I turned my head, his lips pressing against my cold cheek.

He pulled back, a look of hurt crossing his face. Straightening up to his full height, he frowned down at me. "Is everything okay?" he asked, sounding hesitant.

I walked over to the stands a few feet away before taking a seat. Johnny sat next to me, taking my hand. I let him, squeezing his hand in response.

"I was told something today and I..." My voice shook,

dreading this conversation. "I just need to hear it from you."

He nodded his head, looking tense. His hair was soaked in sweat and this wasn't the perfect location to do this, but I had to know. I couldn't go home with no answers.

"Did you have sex with Lucy?" My eyes filled with tears, but I was determined not to cry. Not here. "Before me?"

He sighed, looking away from me. His fingers tightened around mine. His face was filled with disappointment and regret.

I sobbed, the tears spilling from my eyes. I yanked my hand back and stood. "How could you?" My chest felt tight and the tears were flowing. I was so angry. At her. At him. Most of all at myself for believing him. "How could you lie to me?"

"Tillie, I..." He got up, beginning to spew what was no doubt excuses for his behavior.

I didn't give him the chance. My hand shot out, slapping him across the face. I wanted to hurt him. Make him hurt like he had hurt me. I just didn't have the energy. I could feel the stares of every single person on that field, but I couldn't care right now.

I was numb. I was broken.

"It didn't mean anything. I swear it didn't. It was just sex."

"I don't care that you had sex with her. You've slept with half of the town!" I shrieked at him. "What matters," I sobbed, "Is that I asked you to be truthful and you told me you hadn't. You knew, and you still lied to me."

He looked defeated. He knew what it meant to lie to me and yet he had still done it.

"I loved you." I wiped my wet cheeks with the sleeve of my hoodie. "So much."

I turned away from him and walked home. I couldn't look at his house. That was going to be my home too. We were going to be a family. I was so stupid.

I grabbed my keys, ignoring the additional one that Johnny gave me. My hands were shaking so much I couldn't get it to fit in the lock. The handle turned, and the door opened. I fell into Joy, wrapping my arms around her and allowing the tears to fully fall, finally allowing myself to break.

She led us over to the sofa, sitting down and pulling me tighter to her. I continued crying into her shoulder.

"Tillie," Bex whispered from behind me, rubbing circles in my back. She was trying to console me, but it was pointless.

I was broken. Nothing was going to fix it. He'd lied to me and I'd fallen for it like the stupid, nerdy, insecure idiot that I was. It felt like my heart had been ripped from my chest. In its place was nothing, just a black hole filled with hate.

After an hour of nothing but crying, I looked up at Joy. Her bruises had faded over her time at hospital and she looked like she was back to herself. She pressed a kiss to my forehead, keeping her lips there longer.

"What happened?" Bex asked from behind me

I shook my head, not knowing what to say. "You were right, Bex. He lied to me."

"I'm so sorry." Her voice broke.

I nodded, accepting her answer. I couldn't talk about this now. I didn't have the energy for it. Right now, I just wanted to disappear.

Bex turned the television on, settling on The Simpsons. She lifted my legs into her lap, rubbing her thumbs against the soles of my feet.

I closed my eyes, not interested in the program but thankful for the added noise. She gave a good foot massage. If I hadn't been feeling like this, I'd have been moaning in pure bliss.

Minutes later, I tapped Bex on the thigh, getting up, and giving Joy a quick kiss on the cheek. I went straight upstairs, determined to lock myself away. Disappearing into sleep sounded like a good idea right then.

Changing into my pyjamas, I climbed into bed, turning off the lights and pulling the blanket over me. I didn't want to be there. I just wanted to run away. I guessed I could go and visit my father, especially as I didn't get to see him this Christmas.

I jumped in shock as a loud knocking noise came from downstairs. It sounded again a few seconds later, not really being patient. I crept to my door, peeking my head around the corner.

"What do you want?" Bex shouted through the door.

"Open this door, Bex!" Johnny shouted back.

She did as he requested, blocking the route to the stairs.

"Where is she?" he asked. "I need to see her."

My eyes filled seeing him standing there. My body wanted nothing more than to go to him but my heart... my heart was in broken shards, lying at his feet.

"Well, tough shit!" Bex snapped, defending me. "You had one fucking chance, Romeo, and guess what? You screwed it!"

I would have smiled and beamed with pride at the way Bex defended me if I wasn't feeling that way. She would put all knights in shining armor to shame.

"Bex, get out of the way." He squared up to her, still above her height even with her standing a few steps higher than him. "I need to see my girl and I'll move you if I have to."

I would have been scared if someone of Johnny's build was staring me down like he was at her, but not Bex.

She crossed her arms, standing firm. "Joy!" she called, giving him a cocky smirk.

"Now, Johnny," Joy said, bustling in from the kitchen. "Not tonight."

He looked at her in shock. He expected her to side with him, but Joy wasn't like that. She knew that if I had to have him in my face, I'd most likely crack.

"She needs time, Johnny. When she came home..." She shook her head. "She was broken, sweetie."

His face fell at her words.

Well, what did he expect? He lied to me, about something huge. It wasn't something I could just brush off and sweep under the rug.

"I didn't mean it." His shoulders slumped, looking defeated. "I knew that if she knew I had slept with Lucy, I would have lost her before I even had her." He lifted his arms up, running his hands roughly through his hair. "I love her. There's no one else. I can't be without her."

He looked lost.

"Give her time, Johnny," Bex interjected. "She gave everything to you and she needs time to process this."

He nodded, turning his back and leaving.

Closing my door, I went to the window and watched him walk back to his house. He looked like he had the weight of the world on his shoulders, but right then, I couldn't care. I didn't want to care.

I crawled back into bed, tossing and turning the whole night. His scent was all over my pillow and blankets making it ten times worse.

Climbing out of bed the next day, it felt like I couldn't breathe. I had to get out of here. Tossing some clothes in a travel bag—enough for a few days—I grabbed my cash and sketch pad and changed into a fresh tee and jeans. Picking up my hoodie, I left the room, needing to escape.

Joy didn't look surprised when I met her in the kitchen. She just opened her arms for me and cocooned me in the tightest hug. Rocking me from side to side, she pressed a kiss to my temple. "Come back to me, sweet girl."

I nodded, hugging her tighter. "I will. I just need a break." I smiled, trying to ease her worry. "I'm going to go and see the old man." I giggled at the term of reference, knowing he wouldn't be impressed by that. "I've booked my train and he's going to meet me at the station."

She let me go, and, after a quick kiss on the cheek, I was out the door.

Walking down the path, the taxi was idling at the curb. Throwing my bag in the back seat, I looked up just in time to see Sammy standing on his doorstep. I lifted my hand, offering a silent wave before getting in the car and letting the driver take me away, hopefully to some place where my head wouldn't hurt as much.

Several hours later, the train finally pulled into the station.

I smiled when I saw my father waiting. Getting off the train, I grinned, jogging toward him until he was right in front of me. Holding his arms wide open, he crushed me in the biggest bear hug, squeezing me until I felt like my ribs were going to burst.

"Welcome home, darling."

I inhaled his scent, loving the way that he smelled of old spice. He never changed.

"Thanks, Daddy."

He picked my bag up, slinging it over his shoulder. "It's good to be home."

18

JOHNNY

Watching the taxi carry Tillie away a few days ago was the hardest thing I'd ever had to do. Standing at my bedroom window, watching her leave, not knowing if she would ever return...

I shook my head, crawling back into bed, and pressing my nose against the pillow—her pillow—I groaned at the scent that covered it. Strawberries and vanilla.

Sammy came up the stairs and stood at my door, just staring at me.

"You okay?" he asked.

I shrugged my shoulders dismissively, wanting to go back several months. "Not really."

I knew why I had lied, but now it all sounded so stupid.

When Tillie had asked me about Lucy, I should have just told her the truth. It had never been a secret that I'd had a lot of experience with most of the girls around here.

When I was with Lucy, it wasn't anything special. We had been fuck buddies. Plain and simple. It had been a mutual agreement. It hadn't tied us to each other or anything. I had slept with other people and so had she. It had been a bonus when it came to away games as she had always been there being one of our cheerleaders. Towards the end of the previous year, she had begun to get clingy and stopped sleeping around. She'd said she had wanted it to be only me.

I had been a manwhore. I hadn't had the time to dedicate to one woman, especially not when I could get it elsewhere. I'd ended it and that was that. Game over. She went away and that was the end of it. Starting the new year of school, I'd expected it to remain like that. She'd do her thing; I'd do mine. No way did I want to become settled with one woman.

But then Tillie happened.

She'd changed the scoreboard completely.

I had become hooked on one girl and was determined to win her over. I'd just never expected to be the one that would get so hooked on one person. Falling for Tillie was natural. She had made it so easy to fall in love with her. I no longer knew where I started, and she began.

Fucking load of good that did me when she was now hours away from me on her own.

Tillie was smart and strong, but she also wore her heart on her sleeve. She showed her emotions all too clearly at times and it killed me that I couldn't be there to kiss her problems away. She had pulled away completely and wouldn't even give me a chance to explain. Not that I blamed her.

"Well, get your ass out of bed." Sammy threw the ball at me, hitting me on my stomach. "Slouching in bed isn't going to get her back." He walked away.

No sympathy here, I guess.

Getting out of bed, I dragged myself downstairs. I couldn't let my grades slip otherwise I'd lose my scholarship. Sitting on the steps outside, I began setting out my outline for my marketing project. It most likely didn't make any sense, but I couldn't care less.

Looking across the street, I saw Joy in her garden, most likely tending to her green plants.

Setting my book down, I remembered back to the day when we had gone over her color charts. I never had done that work for her. My life had become so centred around my one special girl that everything else just fell by the wayside.

I changed into an old tee and joggers, quickly grabbing the photo of the two of us that I kept on my desk. I smiled, my eyes filling at the memory. I had been bored at the time, so I'd pulled my phone out, planning to take our picture. I smiled at the way she'd turned her head at the last minute, kissing my cheek. I planned to leave this in her room, needing her to have a piece of us.

I couldn't give her up.

I made my way across the street, eager to see her.

"Hello, Johnny." Joy turned toward me, smiling. "I was wondering when you were going to come over and say hello."

"I wasn't sure if I was welcome." I looked up to Tillie's window. "Is she...?"

"No." She shook her head. "You're always welcome, Johnny. She'll be coming home soon."

"Has she... Is she okay?" Half of me didn't want the answer whereas the other half of me was begging for any details.

"She sounded better than when she left. The both of you obviously need to have a sit down and talk." She cocked her eyebrow at me. "And to be honest."

I nodded, taking the verbal bashing. I knew I'd fucked up. I didn't need anyone to tell me.

"You were perfect for her, Johnny." She took my hand, resting it on top of the wall in between us. "I know you can make it up to her."

"I will try my hardest, Joy." I sighed, blowing out a deep breath. "She's all that I think about."

"Just be the Johnny she fell in love with, sweetie." She smiled, squeezing my hand before leaving me to go back inside.

I nodded, taking in her words. "Do you still need some DIY done?"

"Of course." She waved me in and wrapped her arm around me. "I already have the paint. Right upstairs."

I nodded, following her up and letting her show me what colors she'd like where.

A few hours later, the walls were finally done in a fresh, coffee color. I wandered into Tille's room that was full of the smell of strawberries and vanilla, inhaling her scent. I walked over to her desk, smiling at the different sketches littered on her desk. She had sketches of various landscapes and a mix of drawings of the people in her life.

"Johnny!" Joy called up the stairs. "Is everything okay?"

I nodded to myself, taking our photo out of my trouser pocket. I leaned it against her pencil pot, hoping she would value it. I needed her like air and I hoped this photograph would bring her home to me.

Walking back to the house, I took my college work up to my room, shutting the door and attempting to lock the world out.

The next morning, I crawled out of bed, wanting to put off another day of college but I knew my grades would suffer. Walking across campus, I could feel the stares and whispers. They felt like a blowtorch on the back of my neck. Shaking my head, I jogged toward the field, eager to get to practice. Taking my anger out on some of the younger players might make the day better.

Sitting on the bench that the reserves usually sat on during game time, I rested my elbows on my knees. I kept my back to the stands where Tillie usually sat when she came to watch us. I tensed when I felt a pair of hands slide over my shoulders.

"You're looking awfully lonely by yourself, Johnny," Lucy cooed to me. "Anything I can do to make it better?" She pressed herself against my back, her lips right by my cheek.

"Get the fuck off me." I pushed away from the bench. I didn't want her nasty self anywhere near me. "You've taken enough from me."

She giggled, swinging her hips from side to side. She was dressed in her cheerleader outfit, looking as slutty as ever. What the fuck did I ever see in her?

"She's easily replaceable." Her lip curled in disgust. "She never deserved to even stand and breathe the same air as us." Her lips turned into a disgusting smile.

I stalked toward her, glaring down at her. "Tillie is worth ten of you." I shook my head. "I'm the one that never deserved her."

I turned away, grabbing my helmet and running on to the field, spending the next hour doing plays and tackles.

Walking from the showers, I stood by my locker, grabbing my watch. The muscles in my back were aching, but that training session was needed.

My phone beeped with a simple text message from Bex. She hadn't spoken to me since sending me on my way the night before Tillie left home.

She's home

That one message sent a thrill of excitement through me before the nerves quickly followed. She may have been home but that didn't mean she wanted me anywhere near her. I would do whatever it would take to get her to talk to me, but it had to be on her terms. I'd put her through enough shit and I just needed her to talk to me.

I didn't bother replying. What could I say that would make it right? Nothing. Changing into my tee and jeans, I tossed my wet towel into the hamper and grabbed my bag.

After the walk home, I chuckled when I saw Sammy and Logan make their way across the street to Joy's. A shot of jealousy went through me. I had no right to be jealous of the boys getting to see her. They weren't the ones who'd fucked up their only chance with their dream girl.

Walking inside, I boiled some rice, grilling some chicken to go with it. Sitting in the kitchen, I looked over the plays for the next game scribbled in my book. I was trying to get the coach to give Sammy and Logan a chance on the field. Chunk felt they needed more practice, but I hoped that I was slowly getting through to him.

About an hour later, the front door slammed before Logan's laughter echoed through to the kitchen. I grinned at him. He was so relaxed and carefree. I'd kill to be more like that.

Flicking through my law text book, I looked up at Sammy before going back to my notes. Keeping to myself would make sure I wouldn't ask for details like a desperate man. Right?

Logan uncapped a few bottles of beer, putting one on the table for me.

I took a few gulps, hoping it would ease some of the tension. It didn't. I still felt knots deep in my shoulders.

"This is for you," Sammy said, hesitantly. He placed an envelope on the table with my name written in Tillie's cursive handwriting. My hand shook as I picked it up. He patted me on the shoulder and left the room.

Collecting my stuff, I went up to my room, shutting the door.

Opening the letter, I took a deep breath before reading her words.

"Johnny. I'm sorry I left town so abruptly and without saying goodbye. I felt like I

couldn't breathe. The thought of you with Lucy, it breaks me. What I had with you— what I gave to you—I never thought I would ever love anyone the way that I loved you. You took everything in my life and made it special. I know you didn't cheat on me, but you lied to me. I don't know which is worse. It hurts that it was so easy for you to do. I'm trying to find that place. The place in between. I feel like there are two of you: the Johnny that lied to me and the Johnny that loved me unconditionally. I'm trying to merge them into one person, but I can't. I know we need to talk, but I'm scared—scared that you'll hurt me more, scared that you'll reject me and scared that I'll have to walk away. My daddy told me that if you loved someone, you loved them. There is no wrong or right. I want you to be right. I want to be your missing piece the way you are mine. I still love you. I just need time. Tillie x

My heart broke reading her words. My actions had completely crushed her and made her question everything. I couldn't even blame Lucy. She was a stirrer, but she hadn't done anything to Tillie. Instead, my stupid mouth had.

Standing at my window, I looked across the street and smiled when I saw her sitting at her window. I ached to go to her, but it had to be her. She had to be the one to make the first move. If I went now, I'd only push her away.

Shaking my head, I grabbed the ball she had given me for Christmas and lay down. Inhaling her scent was a mix of pure heaven and hell. I was stuck in between both now. Waiting for her to decide her path was the worst torture of all. I just hope she'd choose the path that I was on, where I would stay waiting for her, no matter how long it took.

19
_____

TILLIE

GETTING BACK INTO TOWN, I FELT A LITTLE LIGHTER than when I left. I smiled thinking back to the father/daughter talk I'd had before leaving. We had cooked a delayed Christmas dinner. We always used turkey and this one had been no different.

I moved the sprouts around my plate with my fork, refusing to eat them.

"Are you going to tell me what's wrong? You haven't been right since arriving." He frowned at me, looking frustrated. "I'm not psychic or female and I can't help unless you say something."

"It's nothing." I shook my head. There was no way I could tell him about Johnny.

He cocked an eyebrow at me, not accepting that answer.

"It's a boy." I rolled my eyes. "We kind of broke up."

"What does 'kind of' mean?" He looked even more confused. "Do I need to get my shot gun?"

I giggled. "Dad, you don't have a shot gun."

"So, what did he do?" He had a serious expression on his face. I wasn't sure whether it was because of the fact Johnny had done something or that I was even dating at all.

"He lied to me." My eyes filled up and I quickly wiped them away. "He slept with a girl before we started dating and he lied to me about it."

"Ah." He nodded his head. "And you broke up with him?" He sounded concerned, but the crazy thing was, his concern seemed to be pointed at Johnny. He stood up, taking a seat next to me. He took my hand in his, squeezing it between his palms. "Sweetheart, do you love him?"

I nodded, not really recognizing this man in front of me. What had happened to the hard and serious man that my father had always been?

"Then it doesn't matter. If he didn't betray your trust by cheating, can't you see past one little lie?" He shook his head. "I will be the first in line to whip that boy's ass if he hurts you, but if you love him—if you truly love him as much as I loved your mother—then there is no wrong or right. One lie doesn't change your love for them." He patted my hand, consolingly. "If you let it, it can make you stronger."

After that there were tears and hugs before we spent our last night having a Die Hard marathon. It was nice to spend time with him, just the two of us. He'd given me an oil paint set and I'd given him a voucher for the fishing rod he'd wanted to get. It was more expensive than his usual rods, but he really wanted it. He had taken up fishing after my mother died and I think it helped him to relax.

Getting off the train, I laughed at the sight before me. Bex was standing there, bouncing on her feet. As soon as I was on the floor, she was on me, squeezing the life out of me. I hugged her back just as tight, happy to be back.

We took a taxi home and walked up Joy's garden path. It was nice to be home.

Looking over at Johnny's, I immediately wondered where he was and what he was doing. Was he missing me as much as I missed him?

Walking inside, I smiled at the way Bex led the way through to the kitchen.

"Hey, Joy, there's a parcel here for you," Bex loudly announced.

I hid to the side of the door, wanting to surprise her.

"For me?" She walked straight past me, her eyes on Bex in the middle of the lounge.

I tapped her on the shoulder, grinning at the way her face lit up at the sight of me. Rocking me from side to side, she laughed, squeezing me extra tight. I noticed Bex on her phone texting someone but no clue who. "I missed you, sweet girl," Joy enthused, pulling back. She took my hand and led me to the sofa. "Tell me all about your visit home."

"It was good. I hung out with Dad and we went to visit Mom's grave and took some flowers." I nodded, happy I had been home to have a visit. "We talked about stuff."

"Stuff like dickhead across the road?" Bex asked.

I nodded. "Yeah. A little." I frowned. "I just want to settle back in first."

"Sounds like a good idea to me," Joy interjected. "Time for some tea, I think." She got up, walking into the kitchen.

Suddenly, the front door swung open and Logan and Sammy came bustling in, laughing loudly.

"There she is!" Logan cheered, bending down and giving me a hug. He waved his ass in Bex's direction. She rolled her eyes, but I saw an unmistakable flush on her cheeks when she looked at Sammy. What was that about?

"Alright, loser. Move over," Sammy ordered. "Don't hog the Tillie hugs."

I laughed as Logan took a seat next to me, letting Sammy give me a hug.

"We all missed you," he whispered, giving me a quick kiss on the cheek. He emphasized the word 'all', causing butterflies to take flight in my stomach. "Where did you go?" he asked before taking a seat on the other side of me.

"I went home to see my dad." I smiled up at him, trying to act nonchalant. "We had a Die Hard marathon."

"Nice!" Logan and Sammy both said.

I giggled at how alike they were before Joy came in with tea and biscuits for all. Bex moved from the armchair for Joy to sit before taking a spot on the floor. I laughed listening to the boys talk about practice. They were hoping to get to play this term.

After an hour of non-stop talk, the boys got up to say goodbye.

"Sammy," I said, before walking over to the corner and going into my backpack. I pulled a letter out. "Will you give this to Johnny, please?" My voice cracked when I said his name.

Sammy nodded, taking the envelope from me. "You're not going to go and see him?" He looked disappointed.

"Not yet. I need to..." I sighed, frustrated at myself. "I'm scared to."

"You never have to fear him, Till." He tapped me on the arm. "He's crazy in love with you."

A couple of hours later, I was upstairs, unpacking. I could see Johnny moving around his room. I was constantly thinking about what his reaction had been to my letter. Was he hurt? Angry? I didn't write the letter to hurt anyone. I just needed him to know how I felt. I was hurting. Mostly though, I was afraid he would realize his life would be better off without all this drama. I didn't know how I would cope if he threw what was left of my heart away.

Walking over to my desk to grab my pencil, I froze when my eyes hit my desk. It was in a mess, as per usual, but there was a new item on it, one that had not been there before—one that wasn't mine.

I picked the photo up, my hand shaking. It was a beautiful photo of Johnny and I. I was kissing his cheek, but his smile was so goofy as we posed for the camera. He looked so happy and so loved. I turned it over, gasping at the words written on the back.

Me and my girl – November 2017

Me and my girl...

Was that what I was? Was I still his girl? Could I still be his girl?

Taking a seat in my comfy chair by the window, I rested my sock-covered feet on the sill and began sketching. I had to submit my life drawing sketch at the end of the month and it was still only half completed. Adding some shading to his hair, I smiled at it, images of our time flashing through my mind.

It was then that I decided to focus on his actions, on the time that we'd had together.

They say actions speak louder than words, right?

His actions told me that he loved me—that he needed and adored me just as much as I did him. Grabbing my pastels, I began adding color to his shirt and the background. I was oddly proud of my sketch but unsure if it was because of the subject or my feelings for him.

Putting it down, I looked across the street, surprised to see darkness was already setting in. I must have stood at my window for far too long as Logan standing on his deck took my attention. I giggled when he theatrically bowed, swinging his arms to the doorway of his house. I must have looked pathetic standing at my window.

Rolling my eyes, I grabbed my hoodie, resigned to my fate.

I guessed it was time to have that talk.

Trudging downstairs, I rubbed my pastel covered fingers against my jeans and opened the door.

"Good luck, sweetie," Joy called from her armchair.

I smiled, giving her a small wave before starting my walk. It may have only been across the street, but it was a hard walk.

"Decided to face the music?" Logan asked, swinging on the deck chair. He had his earphones hanging from his ears and a notepad of scribbles on his lap.

"Yeah." I put my hands in my pouch pocket, nervous as hell. "Is he in?" I nibbled on my bottom lip, feeling tense.

"Upstairs." He pointed his pen upstairs. "You know the way."

I turned and took a deep breath before walking in.

I waved to Chunk and Sammy playing on the Xbox before slowly making my way upstairs. I knocked quietly on Johnny's door, waiting for him to open it. Half a minute must have passed but no answer came.

Did he not want me there? Was he ignoring me?

Doubt started to rear its ugly head but before I could turn away, Sammy appeared at the top of the landing. "Just go in, Tillie. He's been waiting for you." He gave me a supportive smile before disappearing into his room.

Taking a deep breath, I did as Sammy said, hoping he was right. Peeking my head in, I saw the room was lit by the lamp on his desk and I smiled at the mess his desk was in. He never cleaned it. Books were in piles on the other side by his closet.

On the bed was Johnny. He was fast asleep, hugging the football I bought him close to his chest.

I wanted to cry at him lying on his bed. He had bags beneath his eyes and he looked so tired. On the floor where his arm had dropped was the letter I had given him. The bottom had a few wet marks on it.

Had he been crying?

I smoothed the few loose strands back from his forehead, unable to stop myself from touching him. He always looked so peaceful when he slept. He groaned, softly stirring from his sleep. I hated disturbing him, but I just couldn't help myself. His eyelids slowly fluttered before looking up at me.

"Hi," he croaked, looking surprised to see me here in his room.

"Hi," I replied, unsure what to do.

Before I could completely freak out, he leaned his hand toward me, gently touching my fingers. "Lay with me?" he asked, turning his beautiful green eyes on me. He didn't pull my hand or try to force my decision. He just waited patiently, never taking his eyes from mine.

I nodded, kicking my shoes off and climbing onto the bed. He shuffled over a little, tucking the ball behind him, spreading his arm out across the rest of his pillow. I nestled my head onto his upper arm, letting him wrap his arms around me.

Squeezing me to him, he sighed, dropping his head to rest on mine. He breathed against my hair, inhaling me. Much like I was doing to him.

Pressing my face into his chest, I wrapped my other arm around him, breathing him in and rubbing my hand up and down his back slowly. I loved the way that he always smelled of fresh air.

No words passed between us. We just lay there, holding each other and breathing the other in. Closing my eyes, I tried turning off my thoughts, wanting to enjoy this one moment. Just me and him.

"I missed you," he whispered, pressing a kiss to the top of my head. "So fucking much."

"Me too. I'm sorry I haven't..."

"Shh, it's okay." Another kiss. "I'm so sorry for what I said. I never meant to hurt you or push you away from me."

I nodded, accepting his words for the truth. Turning my head up, I looked into his eyes, wanting nothing more than to move on from all of this.

"Don't ever lie to me again," I whispered. It was like we were in our own little bubble and I never wanted it to pop.

"I won't, baby. I swear."

I nodded my head, tilting my chin, waiting for him to kiss me. He moved his lips down to mine, pressing softly.

"I love you," he whispered, pulling back and pressing his forehead against mine.

"I love you, too." I rested my head back on his chest, closing my eyes. Listening to his heart beat had become my favorite sound. It was so comfy. I slowly dozed off to sleep.

Waking up, I groaned when I saw it was morning already. Reaching for my phone, I smiled when I saw a text from Sammy telling me that Joy knew I had stayed the night. He was so thoughtful.

"What are you smiling about?" Johnny asked from behind me. His voice was raspy in the morning and sexy as hell.

"Your brother," I replied, snuggling my head back into my pillow.

"Babe that is not what I want to hear." He didn't sound happy.

I giggled at his jealousy, both of us knowing he had nothing to be jealous about. I froze when he tightened his arm around my waist, holding himself tighter to me. He was pressing himself against me and it would have been impossible for him to hide his condition.

"Sorry," he apologized before pulling away from me. He gave me a quick kiss on the cheek before leaving the room.

Staring up at his ceiling, I smiled, so happy that our dramatic episode was over. I was no fool and knew that Lucy wouldn't be happy that I was back in Johnny's life but that's where I planned to stay. No matter what it cost.

WE WERE on our way to campus and I was cuddled into Johnny's arms, hating the cold air biting against my cheeks.

"You guys are disgustingly pathetic." Logan rolled his eyes at us.

"I don't care." I groaned when Bex nodded her head toward our building. I leaned up on my tip toes, giving Johnny a quick kiss before following Bex. I would have given anything to have stayed in bed a little longer this morning.

By the end of the day, I was finally ready to leave campus. Working through lunch wasn't my most favorite task of the day but it had to be done to catch up on some of the notes I had missed.

Walking home, I smiled when my phone rang. "Hi, Joy." I smiled, wondering what she had been doing all day. I knew she had a church trip coming up that she was looking forward to. I was beginning to notice that she looked forward to these day trips.

"Hi, sweetie. How was school?" She sounded so serious when she asked that. "I was thinking it would be nice to invite the boys over for dinner tonight. How does that sound?"

"It sounds good. Want me to swing by their house and ask them?"

"Thank you, sweetie. Have them here in an hour okay?"

I bid her goodbye and dialed Logan's number. He was the one of the group most likely to pick up his phone.

"Hey, Till. What's up?" His cool and calm voice echoed down the line.

"Is Johnny with you?" I asked. Logan would probably be busy but as long as Johnny came, I'd be happy. Joy was important to me, and I just wanted to make sure that my two most important people here were getting on.

"No." He cleared his throat, sounding a little worried. "He never showed up for practice. I just assumed the two of you were shacked up in his bedroom."

I stopped on the sidewalk. What the hell? He missed practice. I was now standing outside his house. I frowned when I saw most of the lights were on. What could he be doing?

"I—I'll go and check on him. I've been in classes all

day and only now just getting home. Is Sammy with you?" I was really worried. This was completely out of character for Johnny. "No." His tone was deadly serious. "I'm on my way home." I clutched the phone tighter, hearing rustling in the background. "Do not go in there without me!" he ordered. His tone sent a chill up my spine.

I nodded before stupidly realizing he couldn't see me. "Okay," I choked out.

Maybe there was a problem at home with their mom and they'd had to go back. I shook my head at that. Even if there was, there was no chance they would go without Logan. They were brothers. Just as close as blood. Even more so.

I was resigned to wait for Logan—to wait for him to go in and see what the problem was. I would have stayed on that sidewalk and waited but unfortunately, fate intervened, making my decision for me. My feet carried me forward, sending me running to his house before I could think.

"Tillie! No!" Logan shouted down the line before I quickly hung up.

I tucked my phone in my back jeans pocket and snuck down the path at the side of his house, choosing to go through the back door. I was hoping it was just my hyperactive imagination but the chill that covered me, causing goose bumps to spread over my skin, told me otherwise.

Sneaking in the back door, I cringed at the creak that came from it. I got down on all fours, hiding behind the worktop. I remained as quiet as possible. Only silence greeted me, making me think that no one was there.

I tip-toed into the lounge, hating how dark the house was.

I froze in shock when I saw a pair of sneakers sticking out by the side of the sofa. I shot forward, shaking Johnny by his shoulders. He was on the floor, his breathing low and even.

"Johnny!" I hissed, shaking him harder. "Johnny! Please wake up!"

He opened his eyes, slowly and hesitantly. His hand shook as he pushed the hair back off his forehead before his eyes settled on mine. He froze for a few seconds before sitting up, his eyes zigzagging all over the room.

I gasped when I saw blood in his hair and dropping down on his forehead. He'd obviously been hit over the head by something heavy before he went down.

He grabbed me by my upper arms, gently pushing me back to make room for him to get up.

"We need to get out of here." He looked terrified. It was not a look I ever thought I'd see on Johnny, but he kept looking at the doorways behind me too much. "Lucy's here with a gun."

My jaw dropped in shock. I knew she wanted Johnny all to herself, but this was fucking crazy behavior. I nodded quickly, needing to get him out of here. "What about Sammy?" I asked.

"What do you mean?" He looked down at me. "He should be at practice."

"Logan said he never turned up," I whispered back. *Where the hell could he be?*

"Well, look who's here!" Lucy taunted as she walked into the room. She must have been hiding on the other side of the staircase in the dining room. They kept a snooker table in there and it was obviously the perfect place to hide if you wanted to stay out of sight. "I thought you'd never get here." She smirked at me. She clearly knew she held all the power here.

Johnny placed his hand on my hip slowly and pushed me back a little so that he could stand in front of me. I let him do it, trying to make it easier for him. I had faith that Johnny would get us out of here safely.

"Tut tut," Lucy mocked sarcastically. "No need to hide her, Johnny. I have a bullet right here for your little bitch."

She was fucking crazy!

My eyes went to the front door as it slowly opened silently. Sammy stepped over the threshold, his finger going to his lips, urging me to remain quiet. He turned into the dining room, most likely planning to make his way to the other side of Lucy.

"You don't have to hurt her," Johnny defended "She's got nothing to do with this."

My hands tensed on the back of his tee, hating that he was in the way—hating that he was willing to take that bullet for me.

"She's got everything to do with this," she replied coldly. There was no emotion in her voice. Lucy didn't care who she hurt here today. She cocked the pistol.

Johnny tensed in front of me, raising his hands in surrender.

"I love you, baby," he stated, his voice choking with emotion.

Before I could blink, Lucy pulled the trigger and in that exact moment, Johnny was swiftly knocked to the side, his body narrowly missing the damage that Lucy had fired at him. Johnny went crashing into the coffee table. Sammy grabbed my arms, leaning his weight on me before standing upright.

I was relieved for a few seconds before the trigger sounded again, hitting Sammy in his back. My eyes shot down to his chest, gasping when I saw blood begin to spread over the front of his t-shirt. My own chest felt tight with pure emotion and fright before I realized I also had blood on me.

Looking down, my head began to feel woozy when I realized that there was a lot more blood on me compared to him. It's silly to make that comparison but it's just something you notice.

"Sammy..." I whispered, before my legs went from beneath me, crumpling to the floor.

My eyes remained open long enough to see Johnny crawl over to me, taking my face in his hands. I closed my eyes, my body giving in before another bang sounded. Darkness then took me, and I gave in, allowing it to swallow me whole.

20

JOHNNY

Standing there with Tillie tucked behind me away from the gun was pure hell. I wanted to charge at Lucy—to use my brute football strength to knock her down and take that gun from her. I just couldn't. Not with Tillie here. If I moved away and unblocked my girl, Lucy wouldn't hesitate in putting a bullet between her eyes.

I'd take the bullet.

Tillie would go on.

She cocked the gun, aiming it straight at me.

I closed my eyes, accepting that this was it—this was the end of my time with Tillie. I could see Sammy by the doorway and I knew that he would protect my girl. He would take Lucy down and stop her.

"I love you, baby," I declared, wanting those to be the last words she ever heard from me.

I closed my eyes, ready for it before I was roughly knocked to the side, crashing into the coffee table. I

255

looked up shocked when I saw Sammy standing and holding onto Tillie. Sammy and Tillie both seemed to be in a trance before her legs slowly gave way, her small body crumpling to the floor. Sammy followed, hitting the hardwood floor and crumpling into the foetal position.

I crawled over to them, kneeling in between them. Sammy was gasping for breath, but Tillie was silent. She was staring upwards, taking small and shallow breaths. I took her face in my hands before another gunshot sounded in the room.

Logan stood in the doorway, his arm raised with a small pistol in his hands. Lucy was on the floor, but I couldn't pull away.

Tillie's brown eyes slowly closed, her body going limp in my arms.

"No, no, no..." I roughly shook her. "Tillie, wake up! Wake up, baby!" I shook her hard, her head knocking against the floor beneath her. "She's not waking up, man. She's not—"

Logan leaned over Sammy, checking his pulse before pulling his phone out and dialing the emergency services. It felt like forever that it took them to get to us but finally the paramedics were coming in with stretchers and first aid kits.

I rocked Tillie in my arms, my eyes never leaving her face. She couldn't leave me. Not like this. I had only just gotten her back.

Logan pulled my arms, forcing me to let go of my hold of her.

The paramedics muttered some stats back and forth

to each other before lifting her and Sammy both on to stretchers and taking them out of the house.

I followed them, needing to go with Tillie, but they shook their heads at me forcefully. She was too critical, and they needed the space to work on her. The ambulances pulled away, their lights flashing in our dark street, carrying the two pieces of my heart with them. My knees crumpled, hitting the hard road below me.

I fisted my hand in my hair, defeated on the cold floor. I wanted to be with Tillie and I needed to be with Sammy. I sobbed, not knowing what to do. Not knowing where to go. Blue lights flashed down our street, two vehicles coming to a stop in the middle of the road.

Logan ran up to the first car, explaining who he was and what had happened all together. The officers from the other car went straight past me, going inside the house. Logan gave me a quick head nod, pointing at the car he was standing beside.

Once we were inside, the officers drove us straight to the hospital.

Thankfully, one of them had the sense to come in with us and take us through the emergency department. Tillie and Sammy had both been taken straight to surgery to remove the bullets from them.

Sitting in the waiting room was pure hell.

A few hours later, my patience was wound tight. I needed to know what was happening. Was she alive? Was Sammy as critical as Tillie seemed to be? Sammy had at least been conscious when the ambulance had taken him away from the house.

I sat there on my own for an hour, during which time

I paced the floor and stared at the door, completely forgetting about Joy. She must have been worried sick. Logan was with Sammy; I didn't want him alone.

Still I had heard nothing.

I shot back in my seat when I heard a male voice shouting Tillie's name in the foyer.

"Tillie! Tillie! Where is my daughter?"

I walked out into the corridor and saw an older man with brown hair but grey on the sides looking exactly how I felt. His eyes met mine before he ran up to me.

"Are you Johnny?" He looked angrily at me. As he should. It was my fault his little girl was lying in surgery with a bullet in her chest right now. "Where's my baby girl, Johnny?"

I didn't even have a chance to say anything before two nurses flanked him on each side, pulling him away to a doctor. He looked back at me before pointing at me.

"He can come as well." He looked distraught, but I was glad he still thought to include me.

"Sir, I'm sorry but only family can—"

"He's her fiancé. He's family." He nodded his head toward the doctor, indicating for me to follow.

Sitting in the room with him, I waited with bated breath, both dreading and needing this update. The doctor sat opposite him after the nurses left.

"First of all, I'm happy to say that they are both out of surgery. It was successful, and the internal bleeding has been stopped." He turned to me with a serious look on his face. "Sammy was hit in the back and the bullet punctured his left kidney. I'm sorry to say that we had to remove it."

"Will that..." I swallowed loudly, my nerves getting the better of me. "Is that going to affect his life?"

"It shouldn't," the doctor replied.

I nodded, cringing at that response. It didn't sound very hopeful.

"And Tillie?" I asked, my voice sounding croaky.

The doctor turned back to Tillie's father, his hands tensing on the clipboard in his hands.

"When the bullet traveled through Sammy, it punctured Tillie's lung and got trapped near her windpipe. Her lung collapsed during surgery and Tillie had a reaction to the anaesthetic during surgery. Her heart rate dropped, and she required chest compressions and a shot of adrenaline."

There was no hope in his tone at all. My blood ran cold at his words.

"The good news is that we have removed the bullet, the bleeding has stopped, and she is breathing on her own."

"Is my baby girl going to be okay?" her father choked out.

"That depends on Tillie at the moment. Due to the anaesthetic we gave her, we need to give her the rest that she needs. She is currently being moved to our high dependency unit where she can have closer one-to-one care from our nurses there."

"Can I see her?" he asked, desperation laced in his tone.

"Of course." The doctor nodded, respectfully standing up. "Johnny, you're welcome to come and see her once you've checked on your brother?" He ended it as a question, probably unsure about what I wanted to do.

"Can I see Tillie first, please?" I would beg them if I had to. "I need to see her—see that she's..."

"Of course you can," her father answered me, tapping me on my back. "Let's go and see our girl, okay?" He rubbed my shoulder, trying to lend some support no doubt, but I couldn't feel anything.

I needed her to be okay.

Walking into her room, I felt like my body was going to give out at the sight of seeing her in that bed.

She was tiny.

She had a needle going into her hand and a bag of fluid pumping into her. A thin oxygen pipe went up her nose and down the back of her throat.

I took a seat next to her, gently picking up her free hand and holding it in both of mine. She had a hospital gown on, but I could see some bandage wrapping going over her left shoulder beneath the gown.

"Her body was low on oxygen as were her blood sugar levels, so we'll be feeding her oxygen through the night. As I said, she's breathing on her own, but we would just like to give her that little extra help."

The doctor excused himself from the room, leaving us alone with Tillie. Her father took the seat on the other side of her, stroking his fingers over her arm. He looked over at me, his eyes glistening.

This was not how we were supposed to meet. It was supposed to be over dinner. In a perfect world, I was supposed to take him aside and tell him how fascinating I found his daughter and how I couldn't live without her. I would ask him for his blessing before getting down on one knee for his baby girl. Instead we were sitting at her bedside, praying to the gods of fate for her to wake up.

I spent the night in the chair at Sammy's bedside. Only two visitors were allowed to stay by their patient in the intensive care unit though the day, but Sammy's nurse in his ward had obviously developed a soft spot for him. If I didn't disturb his sleep, I was welcome to stay and sleep in the chair through the night.

The next day, my world was crushed when I went to visit my girl. She still hadn't woken up and my heart broke seeing the oxygen tube hooked up to her and hearing her little heart beat on a machine...

I was broken.

A few days slowly passed.

Sammy was discharged from the hospital with strict instructions to rest at home. Logan had changed all the locks in the house and had also arranged for an alarm system to be installed at the house.

Due to Tillie's condition, only one visitor was allowed at her bedside at a time. It was devastating, but I had to step back and allow her father to be the one to spend most of his time with her. I wanted it to be me, but I had to remember she was his little girl.

I had no clue what to do.

Where did I go.

What should I be doing?

Without her, I had nothing. I was nothing. She had come to believe in me in a way that I had come to depend on. I had gone from being the most insensitive asshole on the planet to being wound around her little finger. Only hers.

And then there was Sammy: my clueless little brother.

Logan had become a wreck since the incident. He wouldn't leave Sammy's side. Couldn't. They had been best friends since they were three years old. Logan blamed himself for everything—for not being there; for always being busy.

I closed my eyes, thinking back to our memories over Christmas.

It had been only a few days before New Year's, but it had been perfect. I had been nervous the whole day, worrying about her finding my little surprise in my pocket. She had kept asking me why I was stammering all the time. I had always been confident around her and I had suddenly turned into a bumbling idiot.

It had been New Year's Eve and I had decided I wanted to take her somewhere—some place where it could just be me and her. I'd gotten us invited to the swanky party at the art museum in town.

She had loved it.

Her face had lit up so brightly when I'd danced with her beneath the stars.

Asking her to move in with the boys and me had been the right decision and I had been so happy that she had said yes.

I smiled, thinking back to that day. It had been perfect. If it were still that day: I would keep her there with me forever.

My smile slipped, picturing her where she

currently lay. My eyes filled, thinking of her. The doctors had tried to inject some positivity into their tones, but I could tell by the way they looked at Tillie that they were not hopeful, even though the waiting room had been busy with constant visitors: Bex, Logan, Sammy, Tillie's dad, my mom, the coach, my team mates...

They had all shown their love and support in our darkest moments.

It was no good, though: she was still sleeping, and I was still waiting to see her beautiful eyes open.

My face crumpled when a final image went through my thoughts: the bullet wound that caused all this. One bullet fired in hate from a gun that went straight through Sammy into my beloved Tillie.

My legs gave way, collapsing me to the ground where I allowed myself for the first time to break.

That's what I was. Broken.

Walking to her room, I jumped in shock when Logan came barrelling down the hallway, shouting my name.

"Johnny! Johnny!" His eyes landed on me. He was as white as a ghost. My chest tightened with fear. "Johnny, quick!" He waved me toward him, turning around and running back in the direction of Tillie's room.

I ran after him, terrified. Praying to the man upstairs was useless now. I just needed her to be okay. Stopping in her doorway, I froze, shocked at what I was seeing.

"Hi," she whispered, her beautiful Bambi eyes on me.

I had no words. My feet carried me until I was on my knees in front of her. I slumped, my head resting in her blanket-covered lap where I sobbed. She threaded her fingers through my hair, massaging my scalp with her fingers.

"It's okay," she whispered. "It's okay, Johnny."

Her voice was music to my ears. It was a sound I never thought I'd ever hear again.

I leaned up, taking her face in my hands and kissing her. I poured every ounce of passion that I felt for her into that kiss. She would never doubt how much I loved her—no one ever would as far as I was concerned.

I took a seat on the bed sitting next to her father. We both breathed a sigh of relief at the same time, making us both chuckle. He placed his arm across my shoulders, giving me a one-armed hug.

It was several weeks later before Tillie was moved to a private room. The guys hated not being able to visit her. The nurses were strict and would only let her father or me in to visit.

She smiled over at me, looking as beautiful as ever. "My two favorite guys."

"Excuse me?" Logan asked, standing by the doorway. "I thought I was your favorite guy."

Tillie laughed at his cockiness, a blush stealing across her cheeks.

Tillie's final visitor of the day had arrived. He had been back and forth several times, leaving more disheartened each time. Sammy had begun to feel guilt that he hadn't been able to protect Tillie from the bullet that had torn through him. I hadn't been very supportive in that area. I had been too consumed by my worry for Tillie, but I was proud of Sammy's actions on that day. He had put his life on the line to save not just Tillie, but also me. He had saved my life.

He walked into the room with Bex following behind him. He was still moving slowly and holding his left side stiff. Chunk was behind him, standing close enough to catch him if his balance went.

Tillie held her hand out to me, silently asking for help.

I stood, pulling her up gently. I walked with her, keeping my hand on the small of her back. She was dressed in her black leggings and her favorite Yoda t-shirt.

"Hi Sammy." She smiled up at him.

"Hi yourself." He grinned down at her. He fidgeted, his feet twitching. I could tell that he felt awkward having everyone staring at him, but it couldn't be helped.

"Thank you so much," she rasped, taking both of his hands in hers.

"For what?" He frowned down at her in confusion.

"For what?" She chuckled, repeating his words back to him before shaking her head. "What you did." Her voice wavered, indicating that she was barely holding it together. "You saved Johnny. You tried to save me." She wrapped her arms around him, resting her head on his chest.

He squeezed her gently, rocking her from side to side and resting his head on hers.

"You're my hero, Sammy."

Sammy looked over at me, his eyes glistening with unshed tears at Tillie's declaration. She slowly moved to the side, taking a seat on the bed in between her father and Joy.

I wrapped my arms around Sammy, pressing a quick kiss to the side of his head.

"I love you, bro."

He nodded his head, not saying anything back. It had been an emotional day, but everyone knew that we were all here thanks to Sammy.

21

TILLIE

It was several weeks later before the hospital allowed me to go. They wanted to make sure that my lungs were back to full working condition. I also required several heart scans to make sure that I didn't have a heart condition. Once I was given a clean bill of health, they allowed me home.

The sad thing was that my father had lost his job. He was basically given an ultimatum to either return home and return to work or they would have to replace him. He soon told them where to shove it and decided to move here so that he could be closer.

I was happy about that. He had already gotten a job in town at the art museum. They had taken him on as their graphic designer. They wanted to branch out more with marketing their events and I was super excited that he would now be here full time.

I wasn't allowed to return to college yet. I had received several visits from my professors, which was so sweet of them. I had also received a bunch of flowers from my life studies professor with a report sheet. My portrait of Johnny on his arena field had meant I had passed with flying colors and he had recommended me for an internship at the museum. Five students were up for the position and the successful applicant would be appointed at the end of the school year.

I was now living with Johnny and the boys.

My first night away from Joy had been difficult. The police had visited me when I was in hospital but had also stopped by the house. They had informed us that Lucy was in custody and had pleaded guilty. She would serve time for what she did, and I was thankful for that. Thankful that she could no longer hurt us.

I thought it would feel wrong being back in that house. I thought it would be tainted with what Lucy had done but I was wrong. The nights, however, were a different story. Nightmares consumed me, and I would often wake up shaking. I tried not to let them over-power me, but I would either wake up terrified or I would be shaken awake by Johnny. The only time I managed to sleep peacefully was if I was in Johnny's arms.

Joy came over a few nights later with her boyfriend to visit us. I was shocked at first and was secretly jealous. One hour with them, though, and I could see how much they cared for each other. I told her off for keeping secrets from me, making her laugh.

Lying in bed, I was pretending to be reading my worn copy of Jane Eyre. Instead, I was watching Johnny move stuff around, making room for all my books and art supplies. He had a super huge closet so there was more than enough room for all our clothes and sneakers.

He shoved some boxes to the side by his desk before joining me on the bed. I lifted my head, cuddling into his side.

"You enjoy watching me move all this heavy stuff around?" He cocked his eyebrow at me, giving me a cheeky grin.

I giggled, tossing the book to the side. I didn't know why I even bothered trying. "You're just too pretty to not watch." I grinned up at him, laughing when he nodded his head.

"That is true." He looked down at me, giving me a cheeky wink.

Leaning down, he pressed his lips to mine. I parted them, letting his tongue entwine against mine. He hadn't pushed anything sexual on me due to the stitches that had yet to dissolve on my chest. I didn't think he trusted himself to remain calm with me. Johnny could be very passionate when we were together, and he was afraid his lust would take over and hurt me.

I pulled back, wanting this to go further but I knew it couldn't—not yet. I was still aching and in some pain. Sleeping in the night hadn't been fun either. My father had suggested me seeking therapy to talk about what happened. Every night since leaving the hospital, I would wake up shaking from dreams of Lucy. Each night, Sammy and I would be too late, and I would have to watch Johnny die in my arms.

Johnny had been a champ and so supportive during the nights. Each one would always end with me squeezing him and falling asleep wrapped up in him. No matter how many times I apologized, he would just shake his head, shower me with kisses and rock me back to sleep.

I excused myself to the bathroom, letting him help me off the bed.

He hated seeing me in pain, but I think he secretly loved all the fussing and looking after me that he was doing. Johnny was a protector and he loved the extra protection duty that he had been doing. He knew I had no choice but to accept the help.

Leaving the bathroom, I was itching to draw something. I hadn't done it in days, but my fingers were beginning to twitch now. Walking back into the bedroom, I gasped, my hands shooting up to cover my mouth.

Johnny was in the middle of his room, down on one knee, holding a small box in his hands with a blinding smile on his face.

"What are you doing?" I whispered. I was flabbergasted. Was he crazy? I had only just gotten out of the hospital. After everything that had happened, he was doing this.

"Tillie Jacobs." He took a deep breath before continuing. "I have been in love with you from the moment I first saw you. I just didn't realize it at the time. Back then, you were just some crazy girl living across the street from me. I had never met anyone like you and I know I never will again. You fit perfectly into my life and I'm confident I fit just as perfectly into yours."

I sobbed, nodding my head at his words. He was

right. We did fit perfectly into each other's lives. I didn't think I could ever be as happy with anyone else.

"You are my missing piece, Tillie—the one that makes getting up in the mornings worth it and the one that makes me happy to come home." His eyes glistened with unshed tears, his love for me shining up at me. "You made me happy for the first time in my life and I can't imagine doing this with anyone else. So..." He grinned up at me, his hand shaking as he opened the lid on the box. "Tillie Jacobs, will you do me the honor of being my wife?"

I quickly wiped the tears from my eyes, not wanting to ruin the moment. We had endured enough of our moments being ruined and I wanted this to be perfect. I wanted us both to look back on this moment in the years to come with happiness.

I nodded, trying to pull my emotions together.

His eyes widened in surprise. "Is that a yes?"

"Yes!" I choked out, nodding my head.

He jumped up, taking my head in his hands and bringing my lips to his. "Say it again," he whispered, pulling back and looking down at me.

"Yes," I giggled, loving the happy expression on his face. "Yes, I will marry you."

He took my hand in his, bringing it to his lips before taking the ring from the box. He stuffed the box back in his pocket and slid the ring on to my finger. Where it would stay for eternity as far as I was concerned.

He hugged me to him, resting his chin on the top of my head and rocked us from side to side.

He pulled his head back, looking down at me with the biggest smile, his dimples on full display.

"Let me take you out tonight," he whispered, rubbing his nose against mine in an eskimo's kiss. "We've never actually gone out to dinner, just the two of us. How about it?"

I nodded, grinning at him like a loon. Dinner sounded like a perfect way to celebrate.

Hours later, I was sifting through the closet, trying to find something decent to wear. Johnny was already dressed in his navy suit and tie, waiting downstairs for me. My hair was done, makeup was on, but I couldn't find something suitable to wear.

I huffed, grabbing my dress that I wore the night Johnny proposed I move in with him. It wasn't too short and had a cute frilly skirt on it. That would have to do. I paired it with a navy pair of ballet flats, not even attempting to wear the heels. I'd only wobble, fall over and break something.

"I'm sorry I took so long." I sulked, staring at the floor. "I don't have anything new to wear." I was pouting. I hated that I didn't look as trendy as he did.

"Hush now." He took my face in his hands, pulling my gaze up to his. "You look stunning." He pressed a soft kiss to my lips before helping me slip my thin jacket on and leading me from the house into a waiting taxi.

"So where are you taking me?" I was excited. I'd never been wined and dined before.

Looking down at my ring, I wanted to pinch myself. I couldn't believe he had planned all of this. The ring was beautiful—not too flashy—with one shiny diamond framed by tiny little stones.

He took my hand in his, bringing it to his lips before

pressing small kisses to my knuckles. "You like?" he asked.

"It's beautiful, Johnny." I smiled up at him. "Simple and delicate."

"The ring was my mother's." He smiled, looking bashful. "Just before you were released from the hospital, she took me aside and gave it to me—told me that she was proud of her boys and how we all stuck together." He shook his head, a definite blush on his cheeks. "Told me that she had never seen me be that way with anyone else and that when you love someone, you love them. Nothing changed that." He leaned down, pressing his lips to mine. It was a short and sweet kiss, but it was a promise of everything to come. Everything in the future that was waiting for us.

"I love you," I whispered against his lips.

"I know." He grinned, rubbing the tip of his nose against mine before the taxi came to a stop.

Walking into the restaurant, I kept hold of Johnny's hand, still not one hundred percent confident on my own feet. He tightened his grip on mine, both of us following the hostess as she led the way through the restaurant. There were several couples and groups of people seated at tables.

I frowned when we passed several open tables, confused. Where the hell was she taking us?

She came to a stop at the back of the corridor, turning and giving us a polite smile before holding her hand out to the right, signalling our table tucked around the corner.

Johnny tightened his fingers around mine before

nodding his head in thanks at the hostess. She politely nodded back before smiling at me.

I smiled back, trying to be polite. I gasped when Johnny pulled me around the corner before coming to a stop. Sat around the large table were our families: our parents Joy, Sammy, Logan, Chunk and Bex. Behind the table were eight silver balloons, all spelling out the word 'CONGRATS'.

They all looked blindingly happy before we were inundated with hugs and kisses from everyone. I laughed when my dad and Johnny gave each other an awkward hug before ending with an awkward pat on the back.

"You look so happy, my sweet girl," Joy whispered, holding my face in between her palms.

"I am." I nodded my head, placing my hand over one of hers. "So happy."

Her eyes filled with unshed tears before pulling me in to another hug, rocking me from side to side.

Taking my seat in between Johnny and Sammy, my eyes filled as I looked around the table. Everyone looked so happy.

After the food was served, Logan stood, taking hold of Gill's hand and raising his glass of champagne.

"I'd like to raise a toast." He smiled, looking down at Gill. Her eyes filled as she looked up at him with love. "Here's to family. Whether you're related by blood, marriage or love, it doesn't change things." He grinned, holding his glass higher. "To family."

"To family!" everyone chimed before raising their glasses.

I clinked my glass against Johnny's before pressing my lips to his.

Logan was right about family.

At the end of the day, family was not an important thing. It was everything.

ABOUT THE AUTHOR

Lizzie James lives in the valleys of South Wales, UK with her family.
Working full time for her local authority keeps her busy but her free time is spent in her favourite pursuits of writing, reading, listening to music and travelling. She is passionate about her writing and cooperatively works with a team of dedicated bloggers through CLiK Book Blog and Facebook Group to advance and promote not only her own work but that of other aspiring Indie Authors.

Facebook:
https://www.facebook.com/authorlizziejames

Twitter:
https://www.twitter.com/lizziejames86

Instagram:
https://www.instagram.com/lizziejames_86/

Tangled Trilogy

.

Printed in Poland
by Amazon Fulfillment
Poland Sp. z o.o., Wrocław